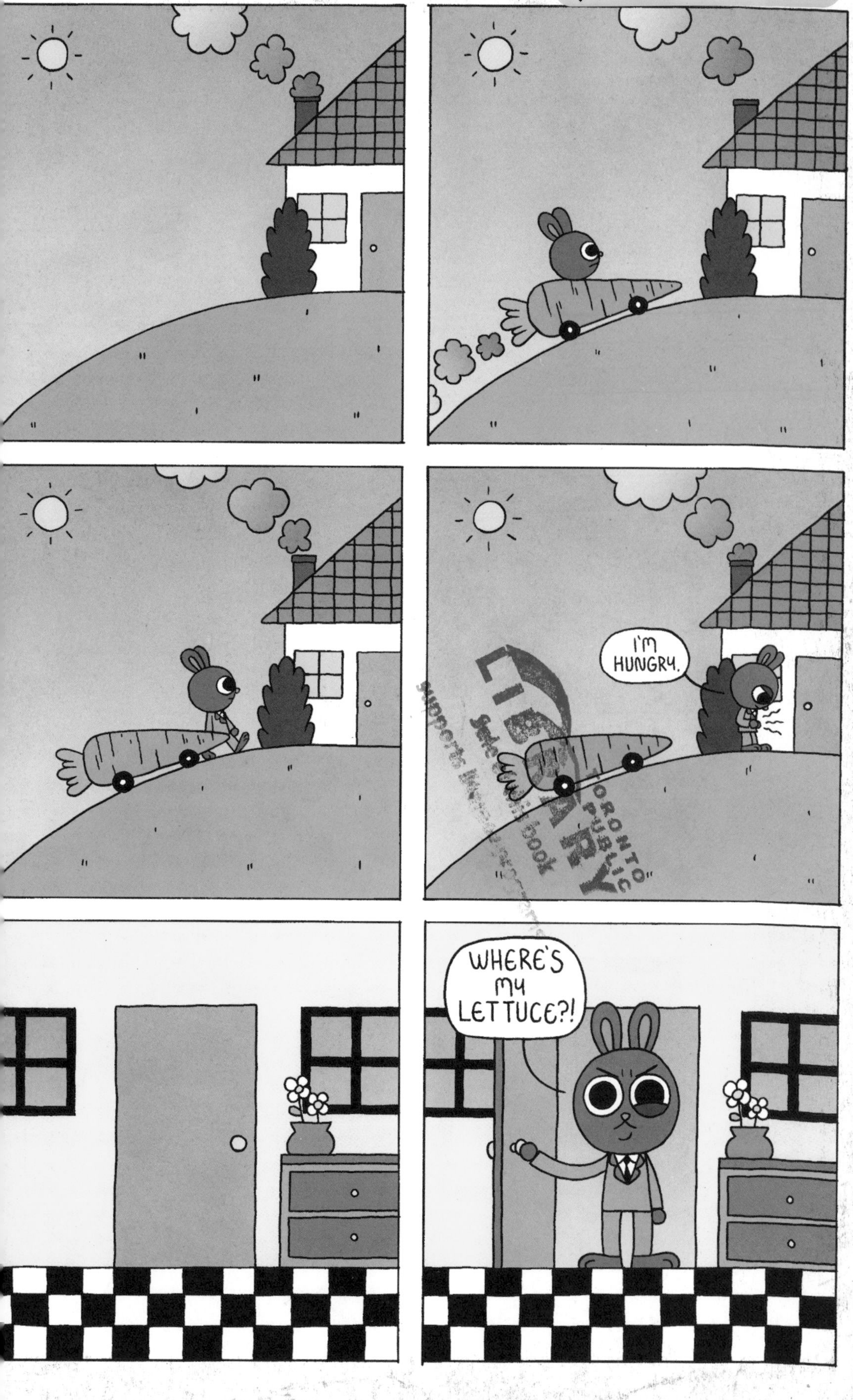
I'M
HUNGRY.
WHERE'S
MY
LETTUCE?!

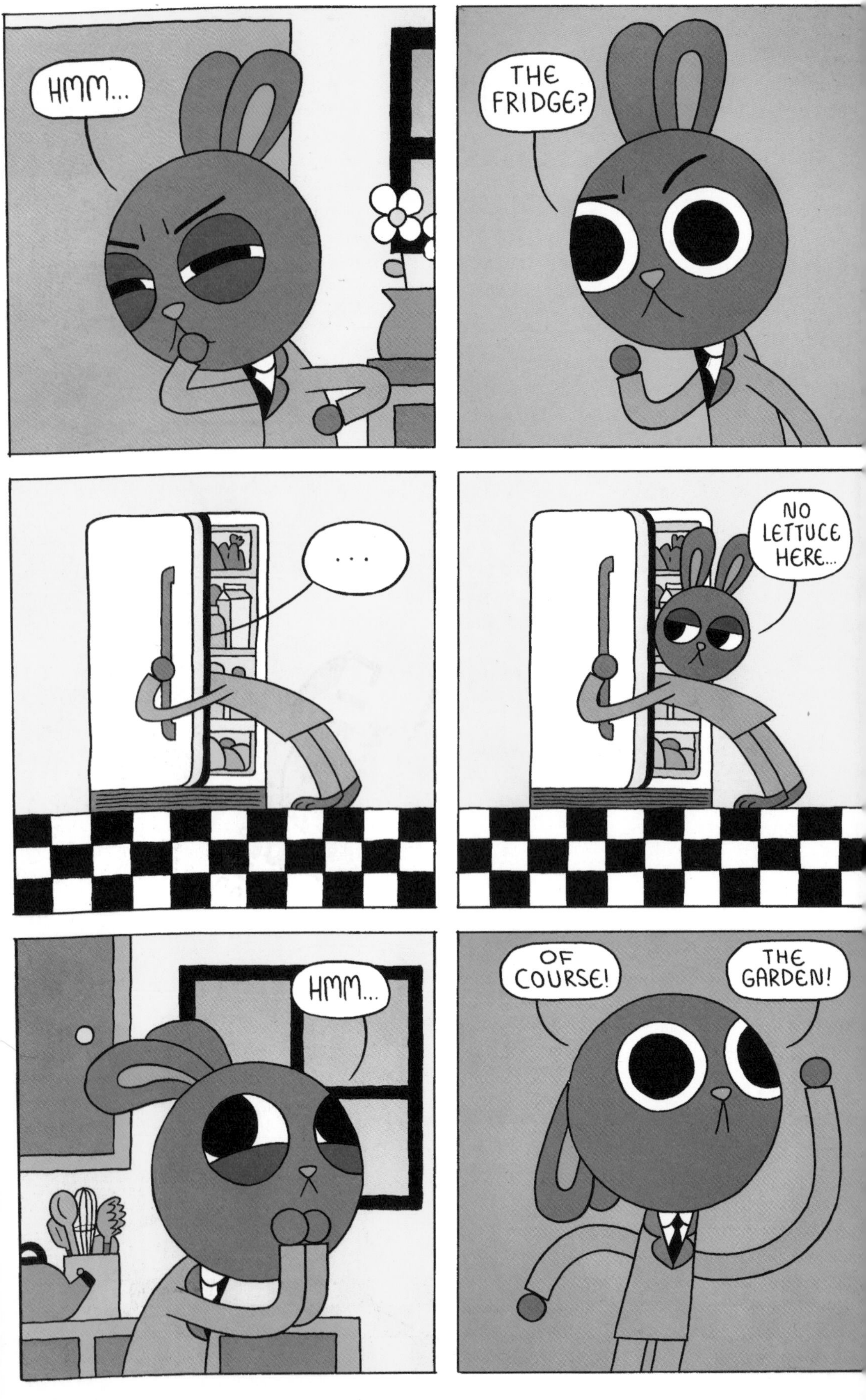
HMM...
THE FRIDGE?
...
NO LETTUCE HERE...
HMM...
OF COURSE!
THE GARDEN!

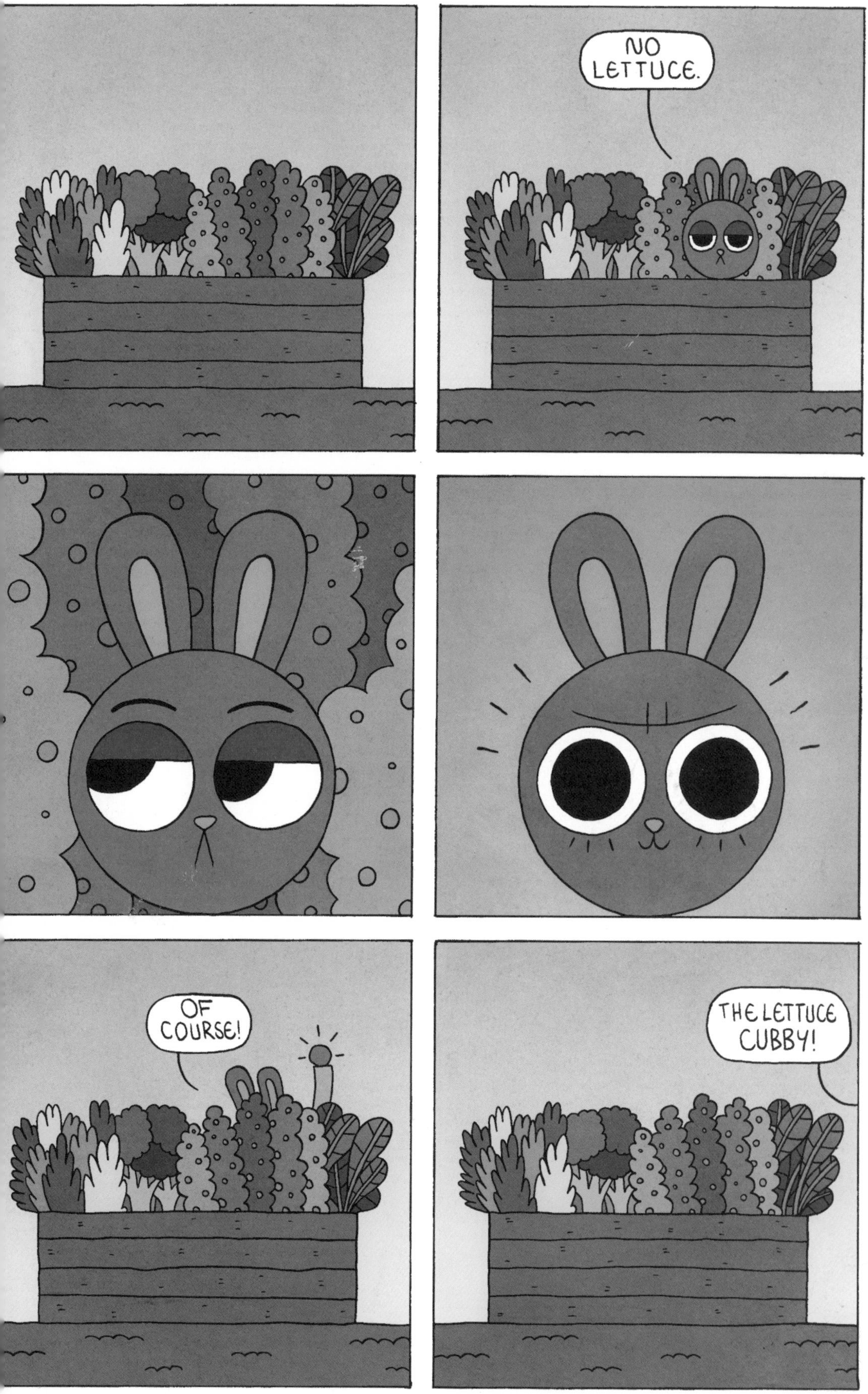
NO LETTUCE.
OF COURSE!
THE LETTUCE CUBBY!

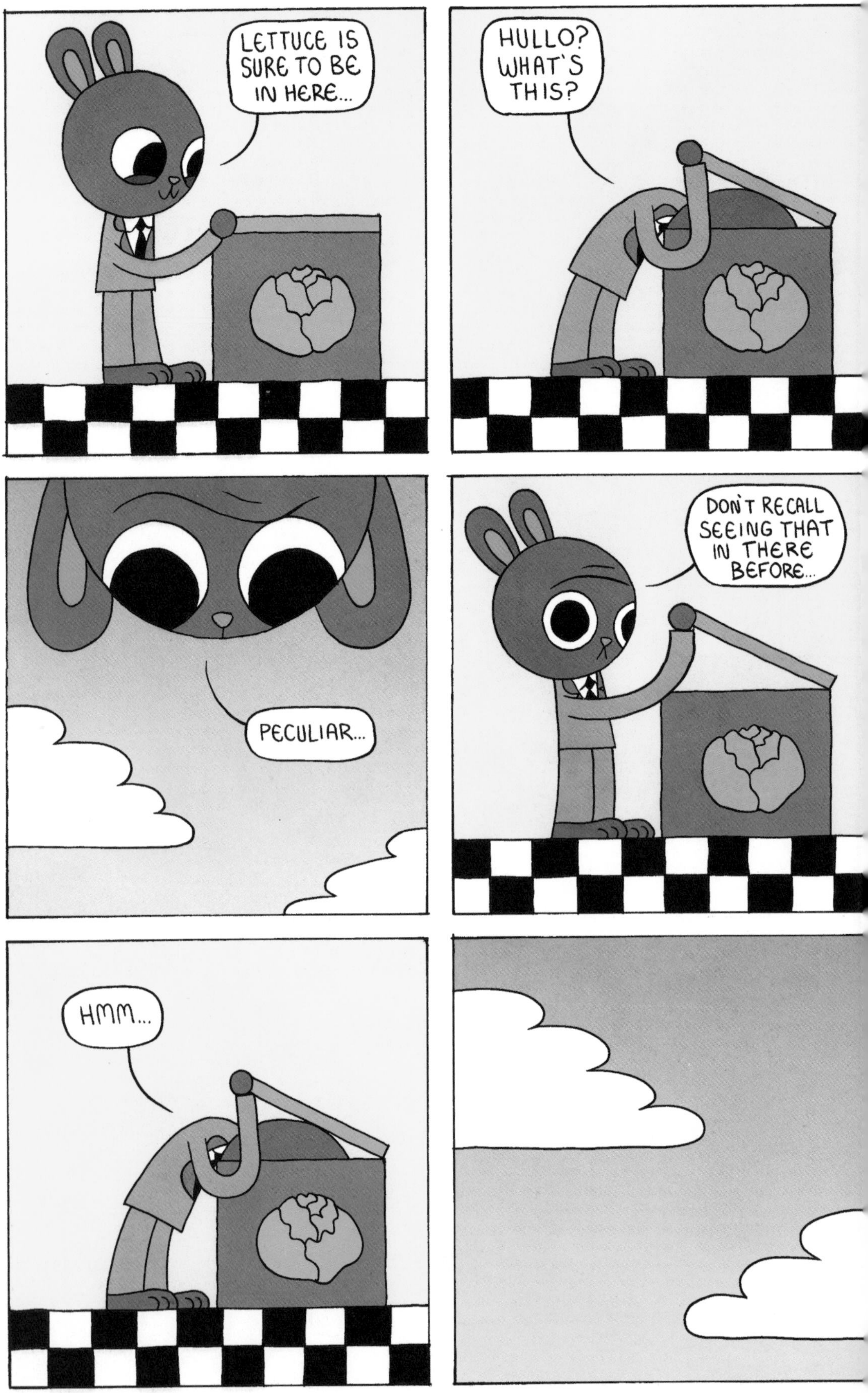
LETTUCE IS SURE TO BE IN HERE...
HULLO? WHAT'S THIS?
PECULIAR...
DON'T RECALL SEEING THAT IN THERE BEFORE...
HMM...

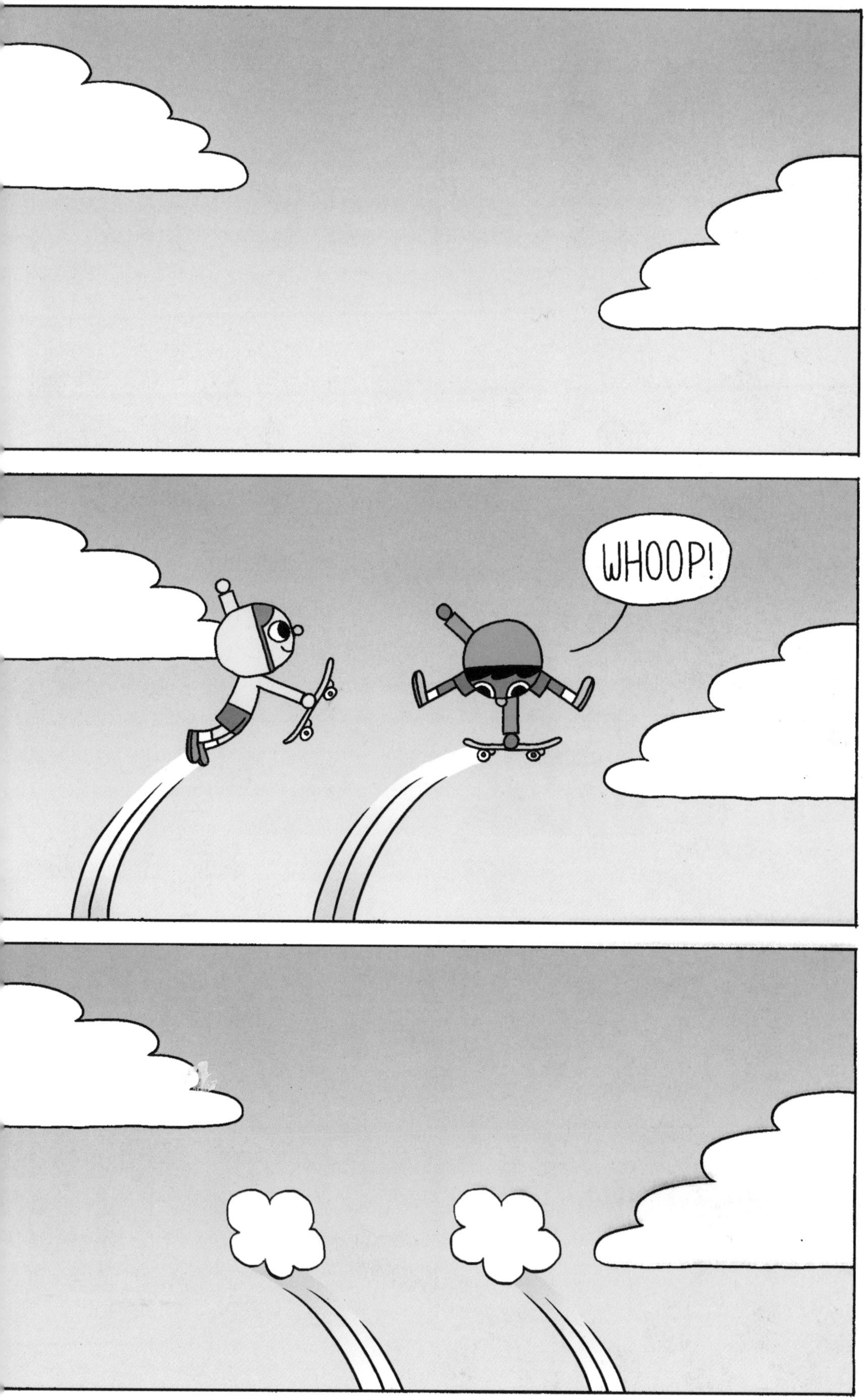
WHOOP!

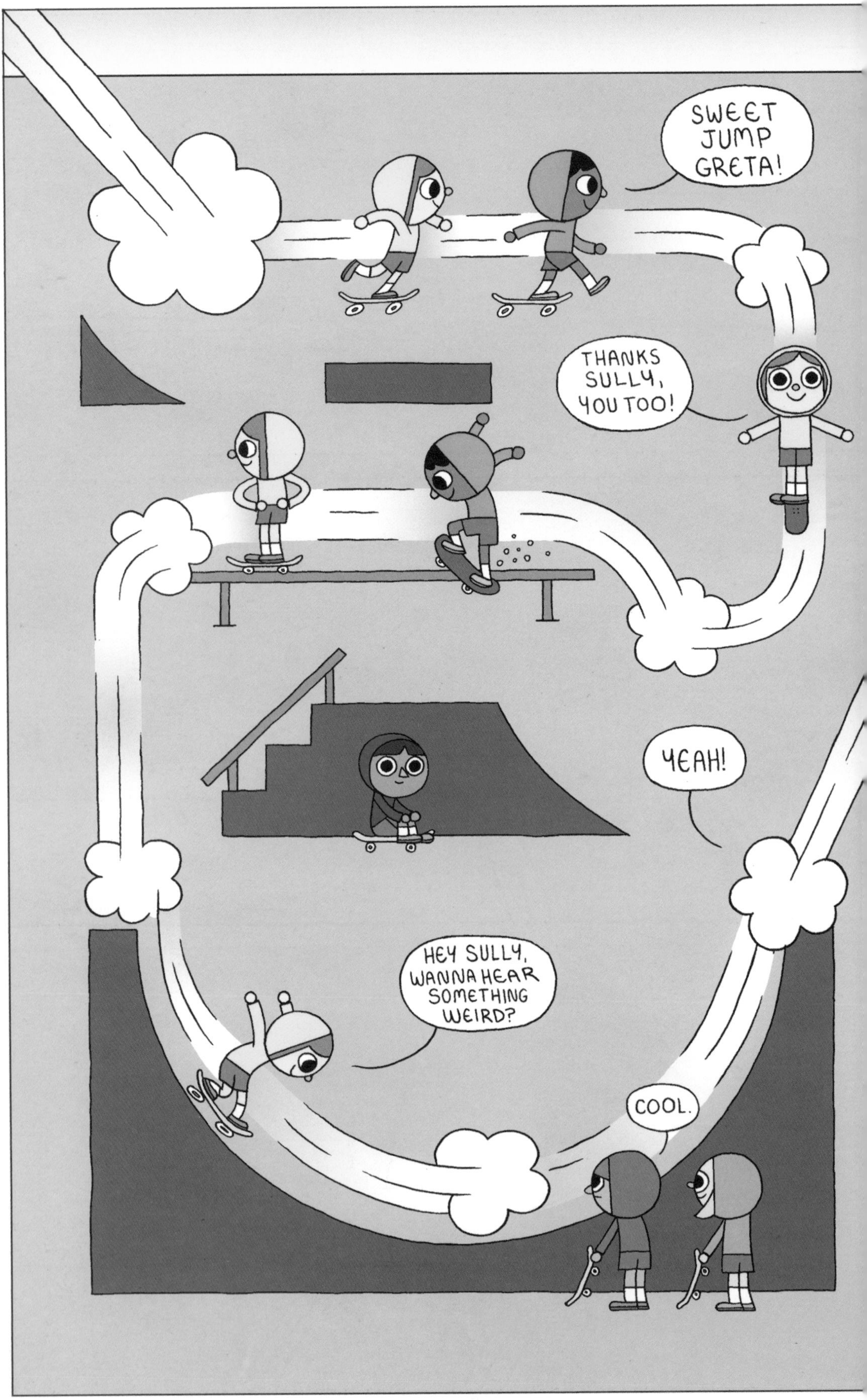
SWEET JUMP GRETA!
THANKS SULLY, YOU TOO!
YEAH!
HEY SULLY, WANNA HEAR SOMETHING WEIRD?
COOL.

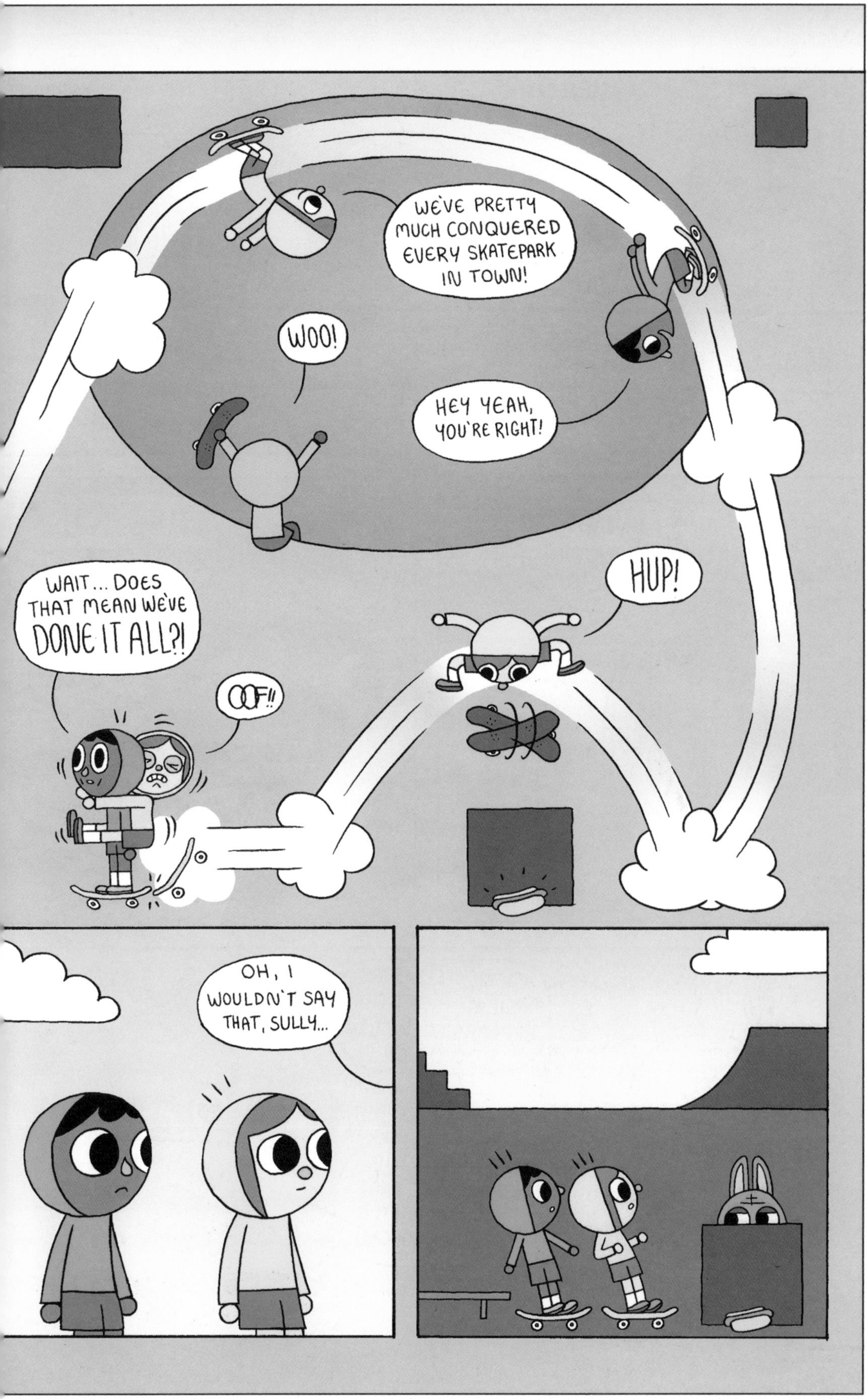
WE'VE PRETTY MUCH CONQUERED EVERY SKATEPARK IN TOWN!
WOO!
HEY YEAH, YOU'RE RIGHT!
HUP!
WAIT... DOES THAT MEAN WE'VE DONE IT ALL?!
OOF!!
OH, I WOULDN'T SAY THAT, SULLY...

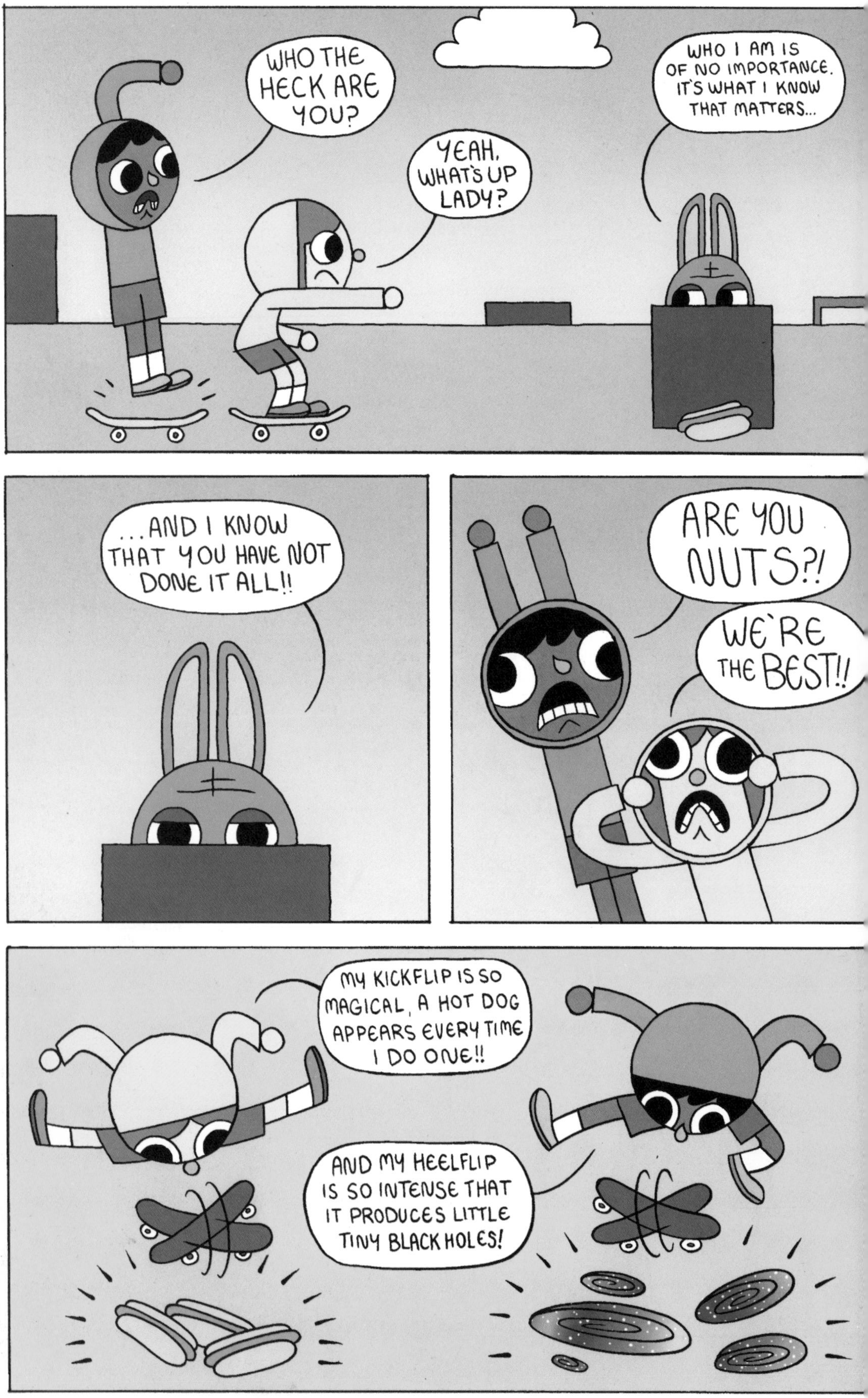
WHO THE HECK ARE YOU?
YEAH, WHAT'S UP LADY?
WHO I AM IS OF NO IMPORTANCE. IT'S WHAT I KNOW THAT MATTERS...
...AND I KNOW THAT YOU HAVE NOT DONE IT ALL!!
ARE YOU NUTS?!
WE'RE THE BEST!!
MY KICKFLIP IS SO MAGICAL, A HOT DOG APPEARS EVERY TIME I DO ONE!!
AND MY HEELFLIP IS SO INTENSE THAT IT PRODUCES LITTLE TINY BLACK HOLES!

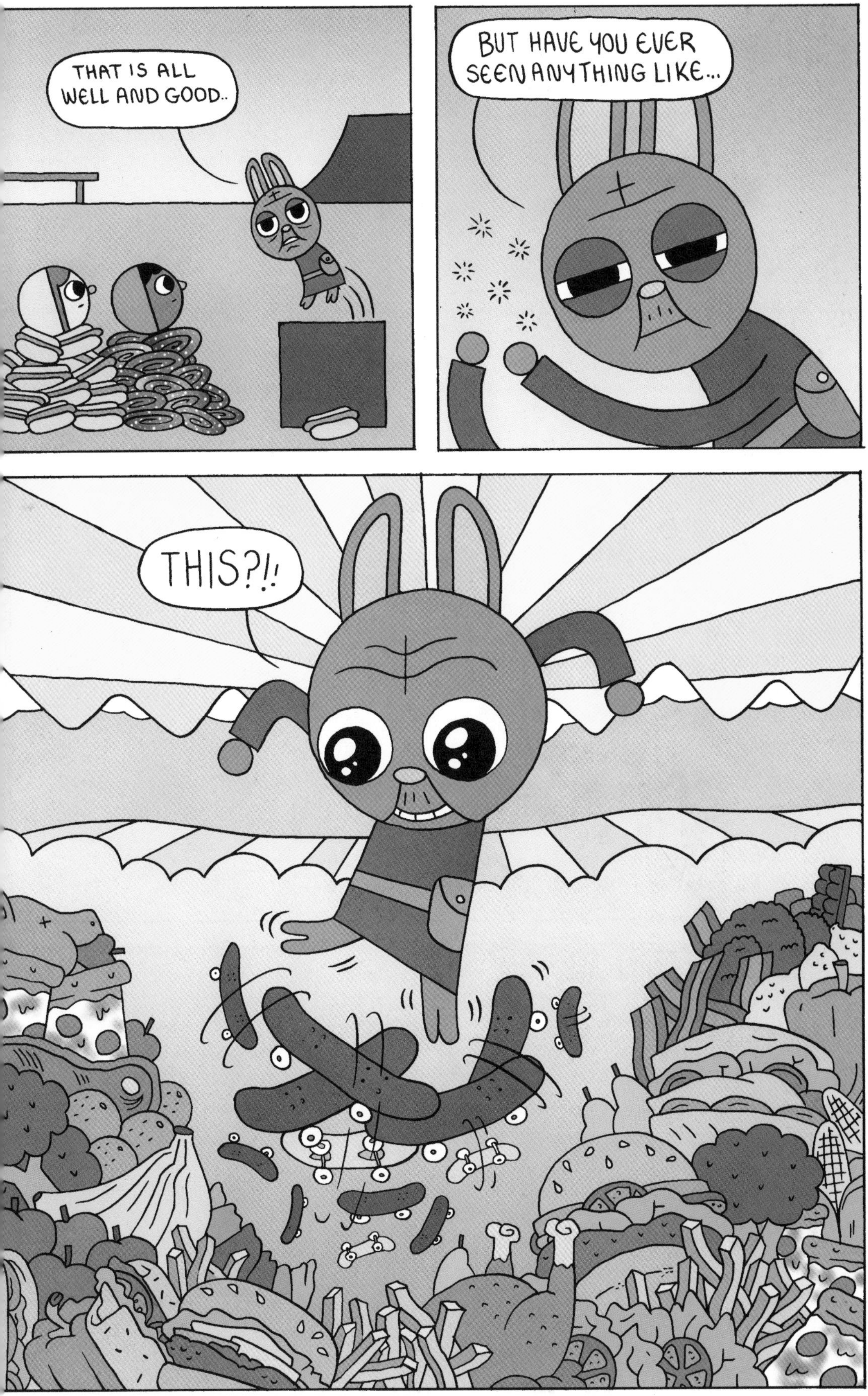
THAT IS ALL WELL AND GOOD..
BUT HAVE YOU EVER SEEN ANYTHING LIKE...
THIS?!!

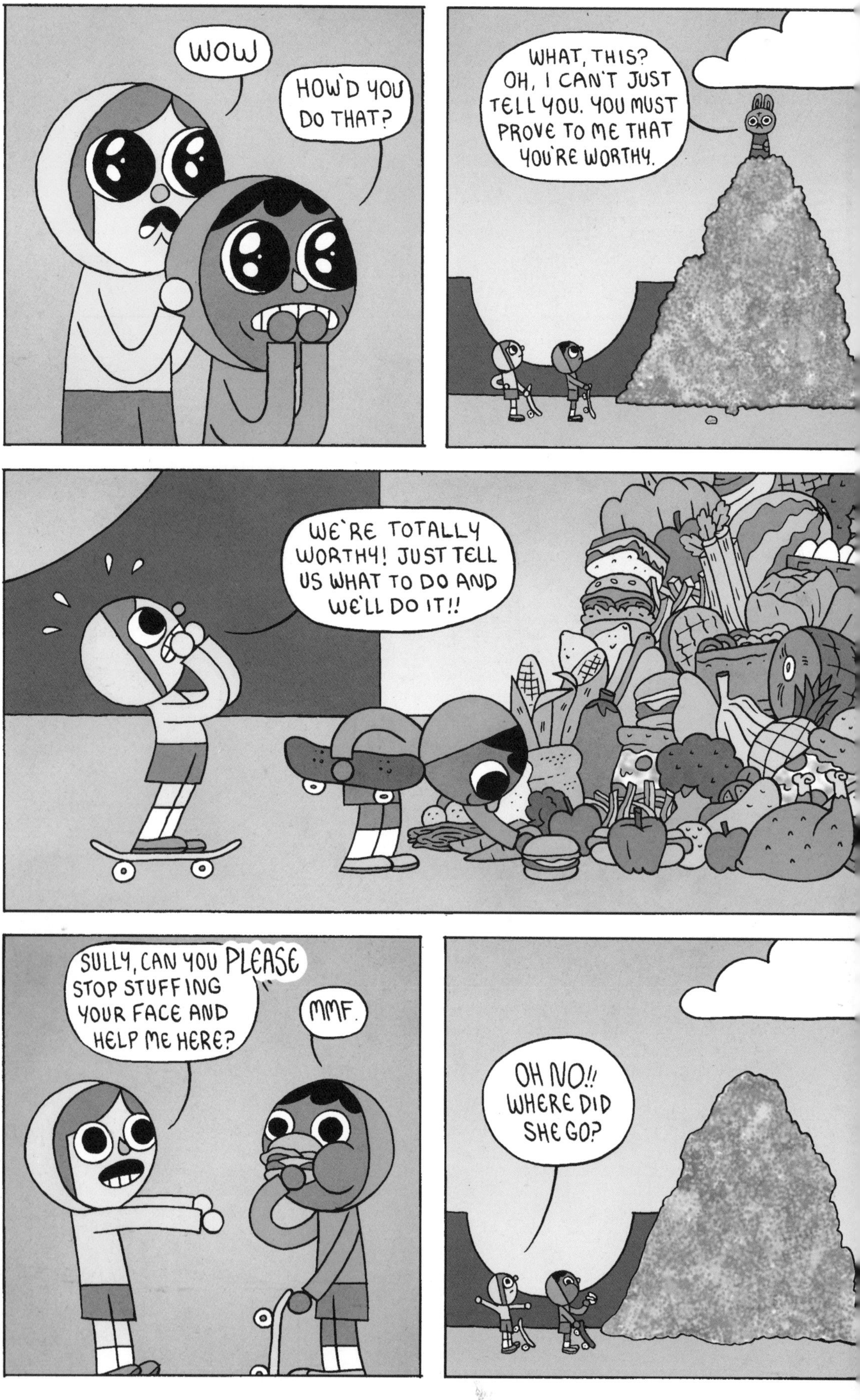
WOW
HOW'D YOU DO THAT?
WHAT, THIS? OH, I CAN'T JUST TELL YOU. YOU MUST PROVE TO ME THAT YOU'RE WORTHY.
WE'RE TOTALLY WORTHY! JUST TELL US WHAT TO DO AND WE'LL DO IT!!
SULLY, CAN YOU PLEASE STOP STUFFING YOUR FACE AND HELP ME HERE?
MMF.
OH NO!! WHERE DID SHE GO?

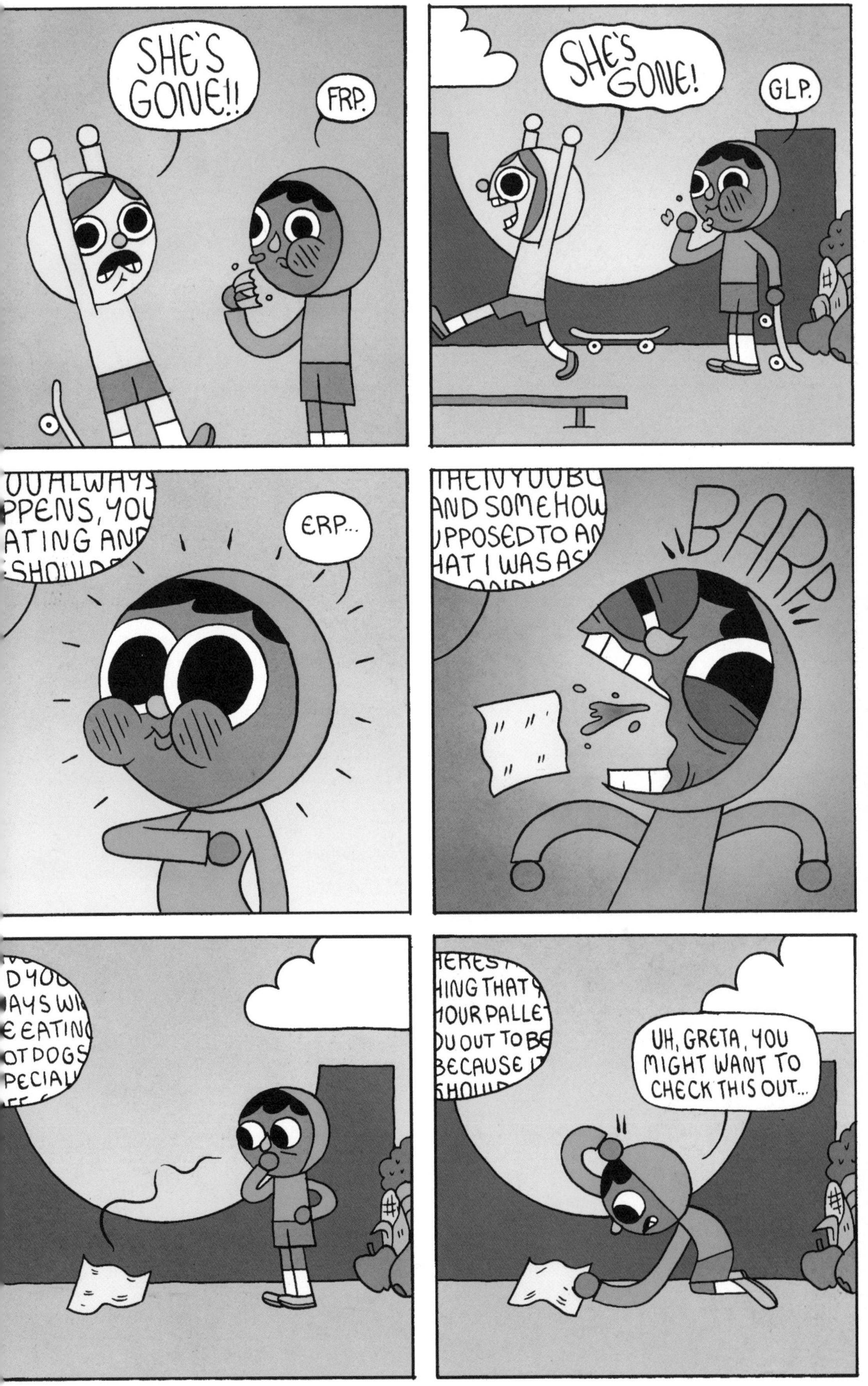
SHE'S GONE!!
FRP.
SHE'S GONE!
GLP.
ERP...
BARRP
UH, GRETA, YOU MIGHT WANT TO CHECK THIS OUT...

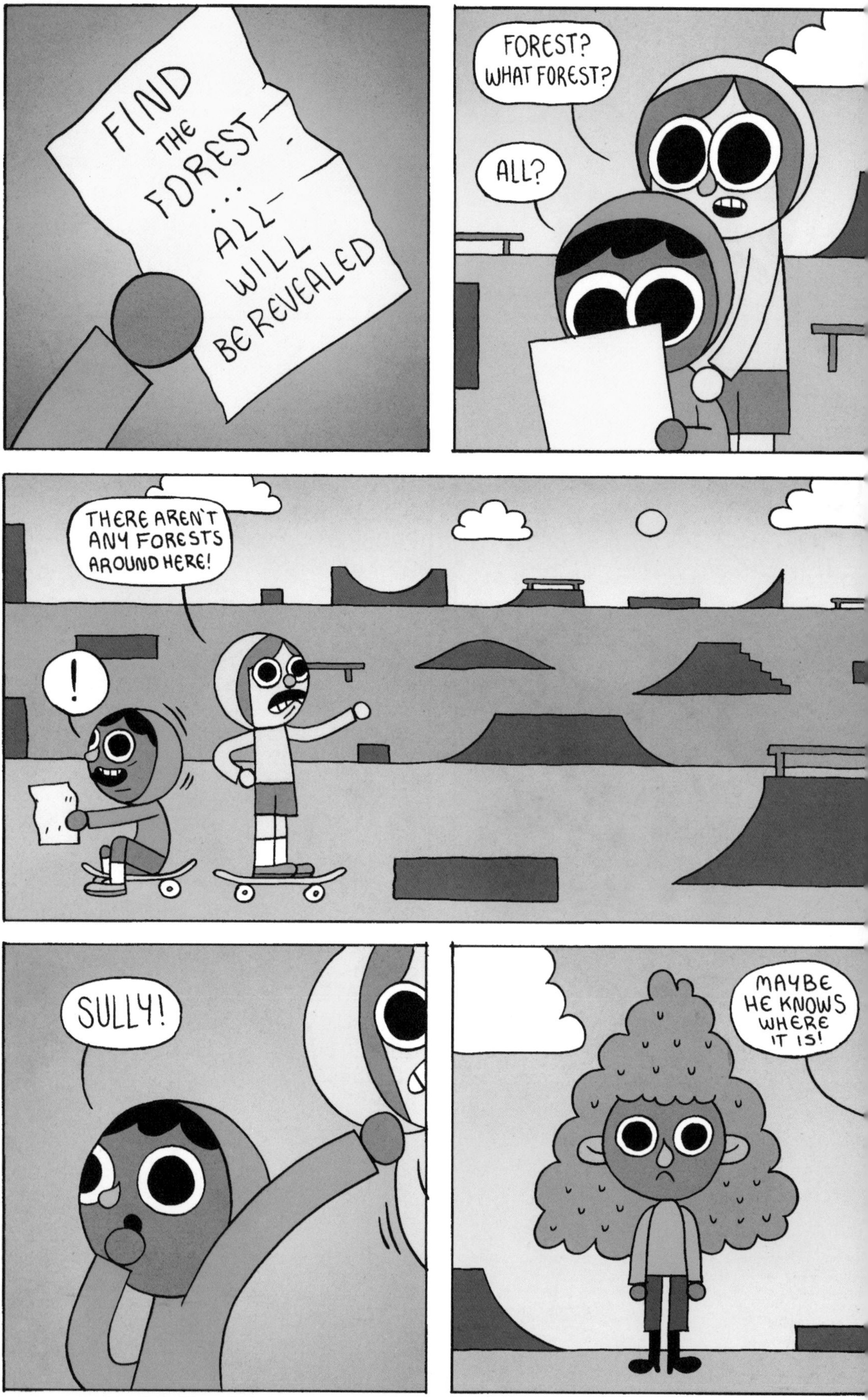
FIND THE FOREST ... ALL WILL BE REVEALED
FOREST? WHAT FOREST?
ALL?
THERE AREN'T ANY FORESTS AROUND HERE!
!
SULLY!
MAYBE HE KNOWS WHERE IT IS!

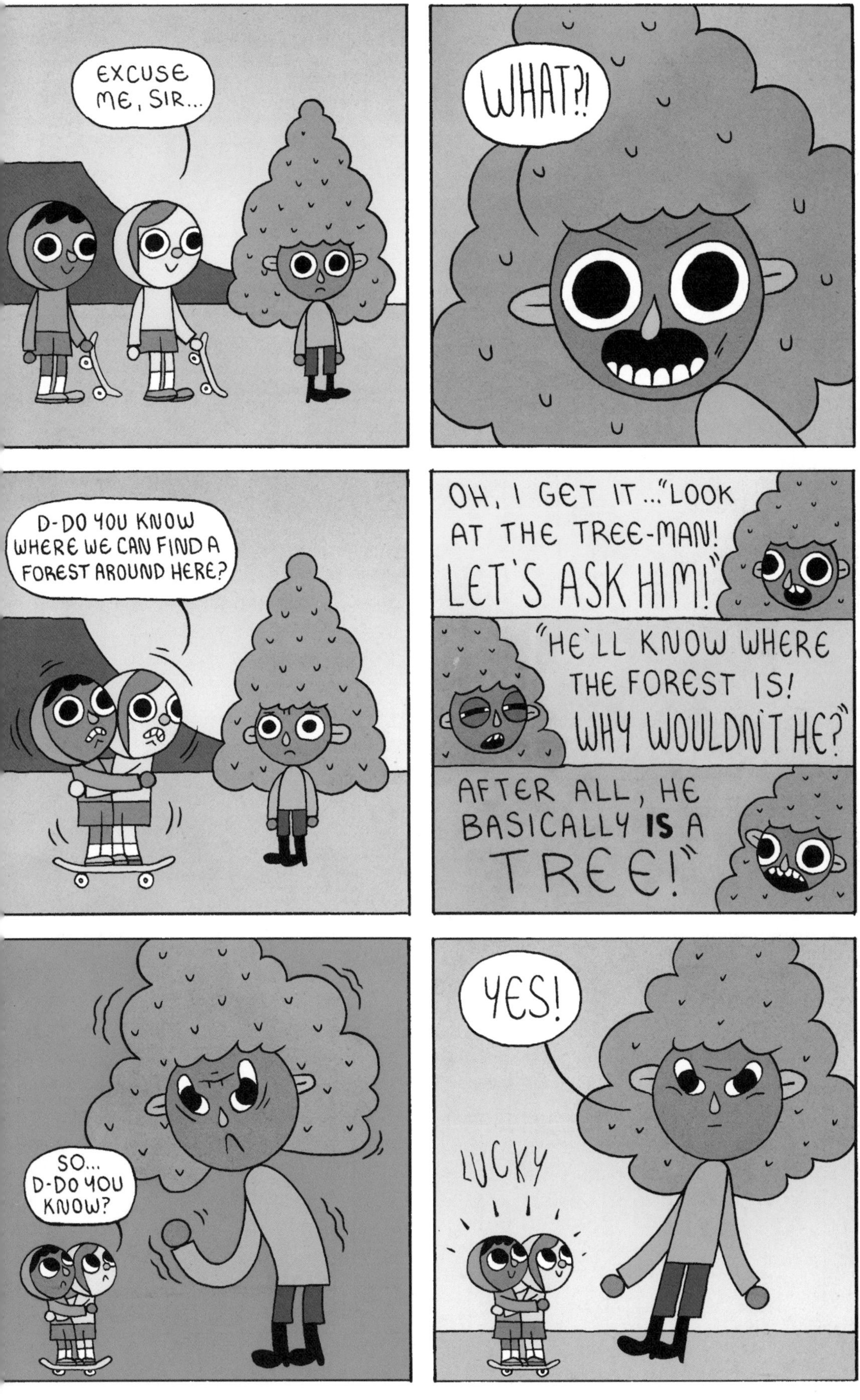
EXCUSE ME, SIR...
WHAT?!
D-DO YOU KNOW WHERE WE CAN FIND A FOREST AROUND HERE?
OH, I GET IT..."LOOK AT THE TREE-MAN! LET'S ASK HIM!"
"HE'LL KNOW WHERE THE FOREST IS! WHY WOULDN'T HE?"
AFTER ALL, HE BASICALLY **IS** A TREE!"
SO... D-DO YOU KNOW?
YES!
LUCKY

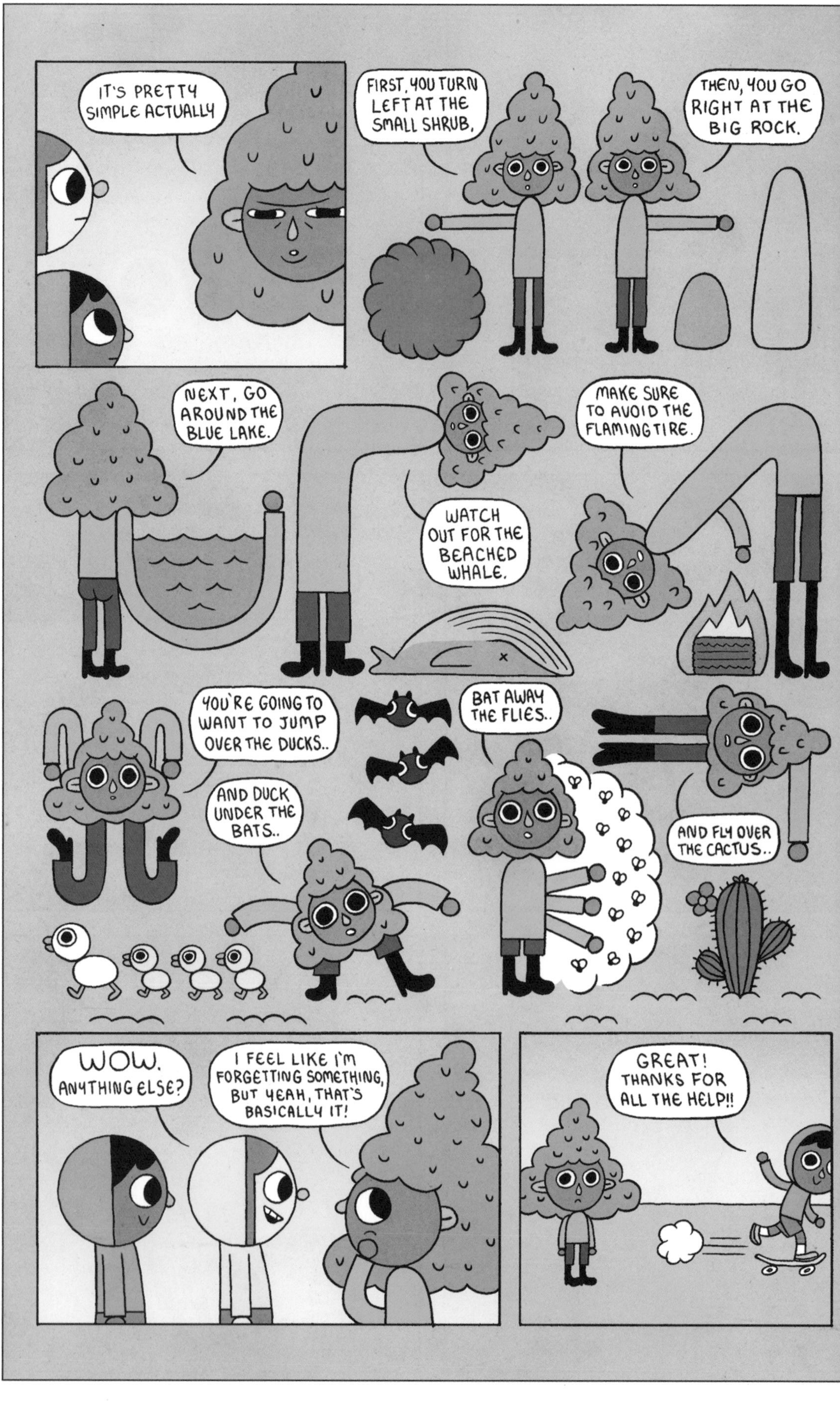
IT'S PRETTY SIMPLE ACTUALLY
FIRST, YOU TURN LEFT AT THE SMALL SHRUB,
THEN, YOU GO RIGHT AT THE BIG ROCK.
NEXT, GO AROUND THE BLUE LAKE.
WATCH OUT FOR THE BEACHED WHALE.
MAKE SURE TO AVOID THE FLAMING TIRE.
YOU'RE GOING TO WANT TO JUMP OVER THE DUCKS..
AND DUCK UNDER THE BATS..
BAT AWAY THE FLIES..
AND FLY OVER THE CACTUS..
WOW. ANYTHING ELSE?
I FEEL LIKE I'M FORGETTING SOMETHING, BUT YEAH, THAT'S BASICALLY IT!
GREAT! THANKS FOR ALL THE HELP!!

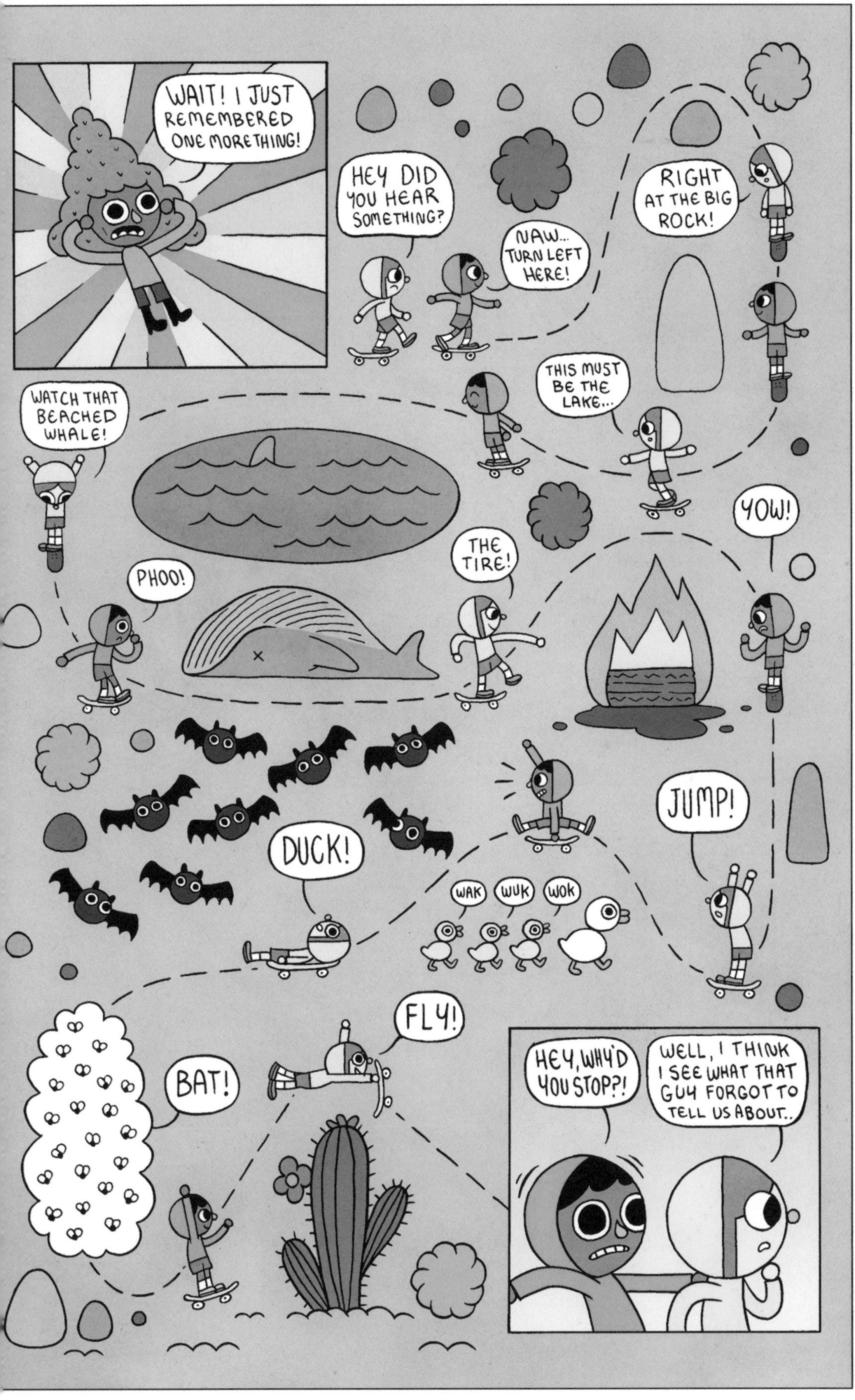
WAIT! I JUST REMEMBERED ONE MORE THING!
HEY DID YOU HEAR SOMETHING?
NAW... TURN LEFT HERE!
RIGHT AT THE BIG ROCK!
THIS MUST BE THE LAKE...
WATCH THAT BEACHED WHALE!
PHOO!
THE TIRE!
YOW!
JUMP!
DUCK!
WAK
WUK
WOK
FLY!
BAT!
HEY, WHY'D YOU STOP?!
WELL, I THINK I SEE WHAT THAT GUY FORGOT TO TELL US ABOUT..

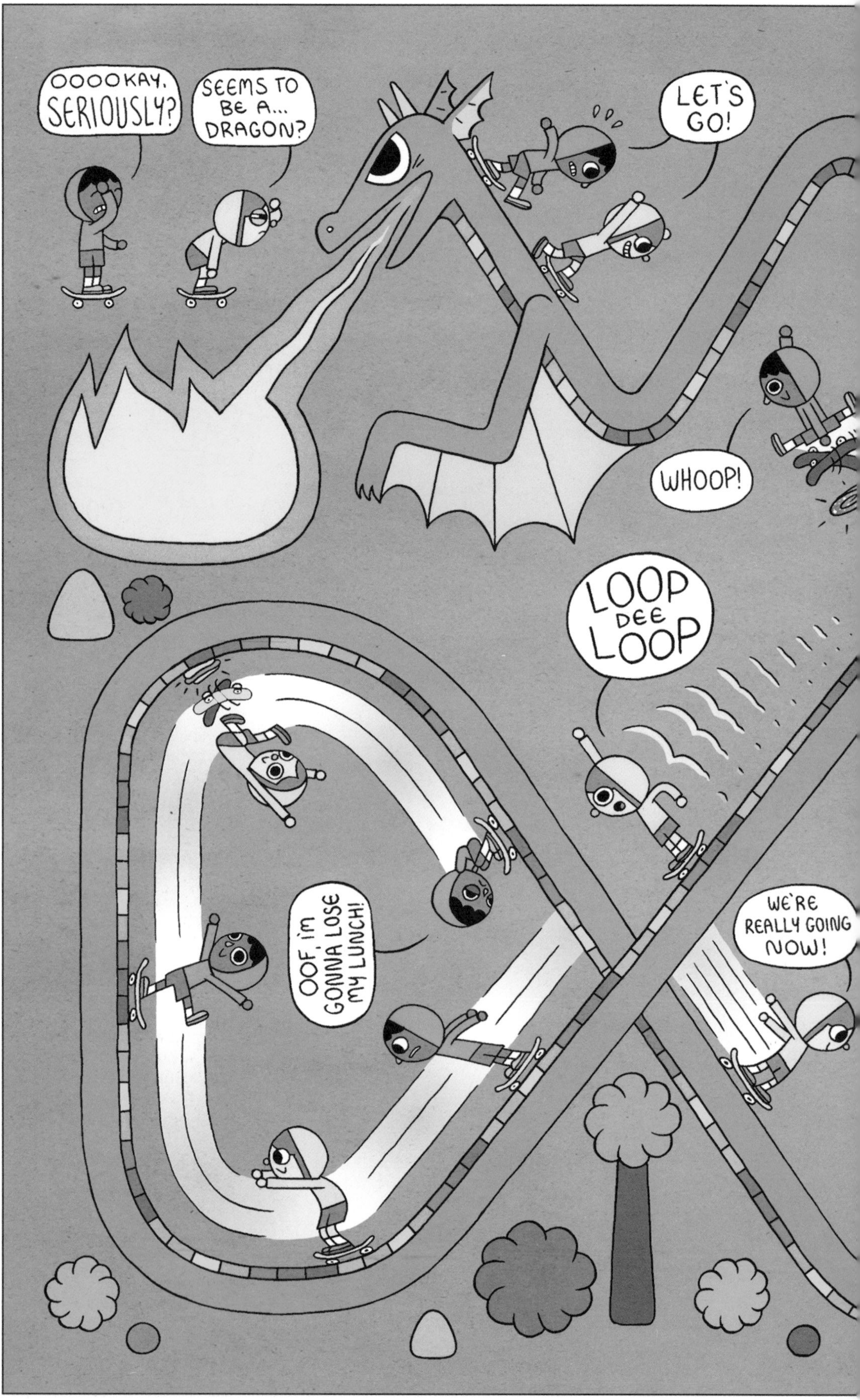
OOOOKAY, SERIOUSLY?
SEEMS TO BE A... DRAGON?
LET'S GO!
WHOOP!
LOOP DEE LOOP
OOF, I'M GONNA LOSE MY LUNCH!
WE'RE REALLY GOING NOW!

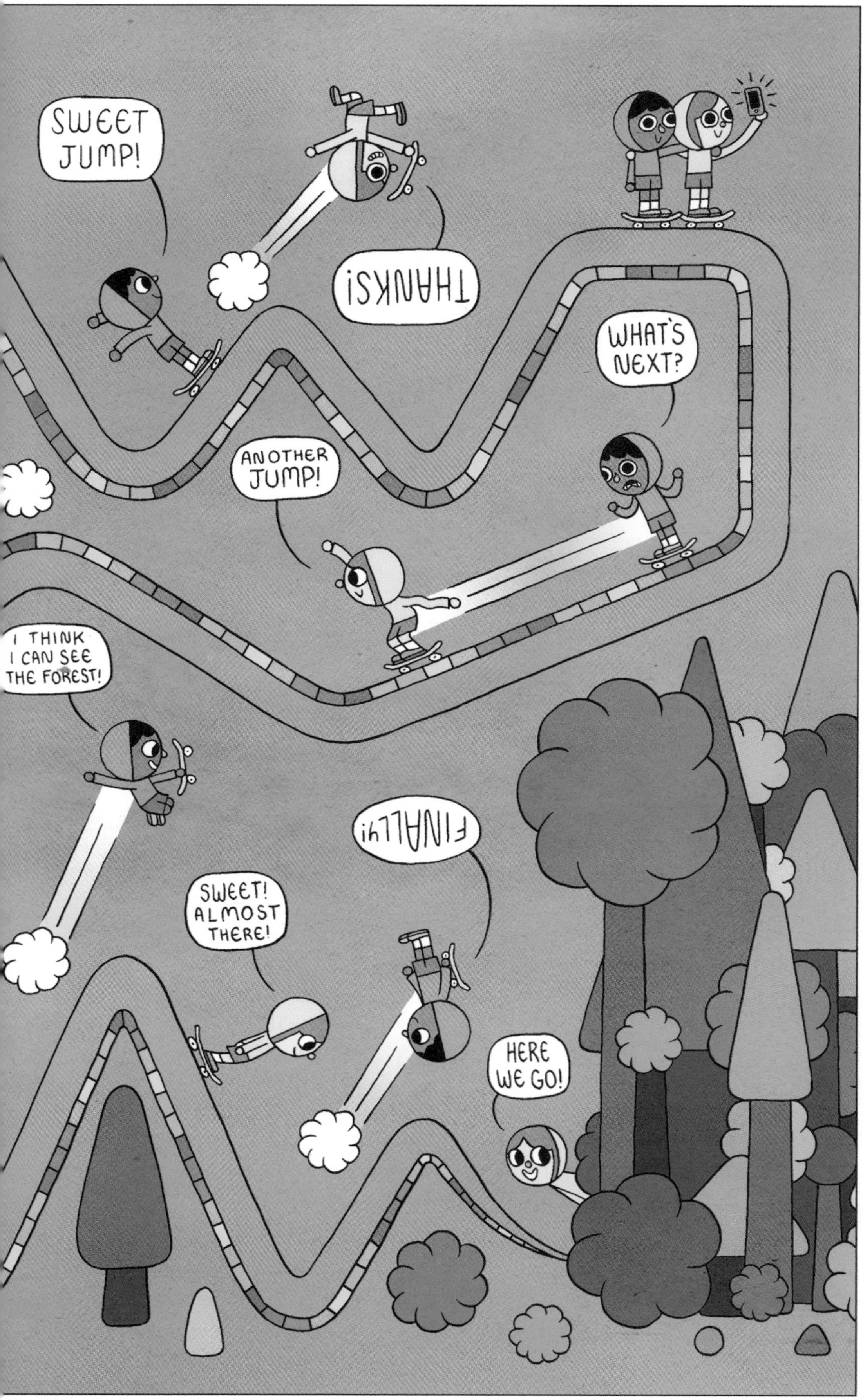
SWEET JUMP!
THANKS!
WHAT'S NEXT?
ANOTHER JUMP!
I THINK I CAN SEE THE FOREST!
FINALLY!
SWEET! ALMOST THERE!
HERE WE GO!

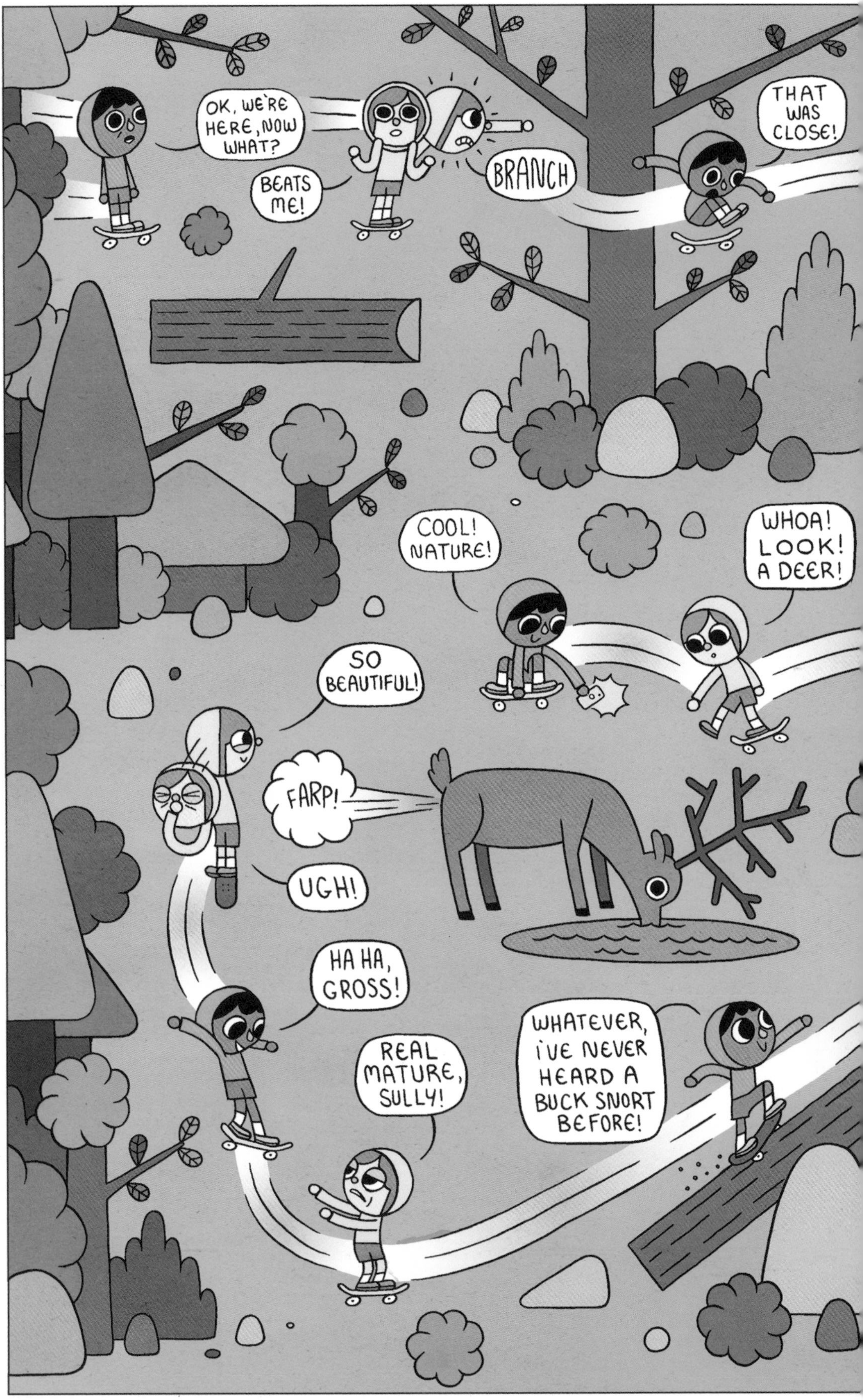

OK, WE'RE HERE, NOW WHAT?
BEATS ME!
BRANCH
THAT WAS CLOSE!
COOL! NATURE!
WHOA! LOOK! A DEER!
SO BEAUTIFUL!
FARP!
UGH!
HA HA, GROSS!
REAL MATURE, SULLY!
WHATEVER, I'VE NEVER HEARD A BUCK SNORT BEFORE!

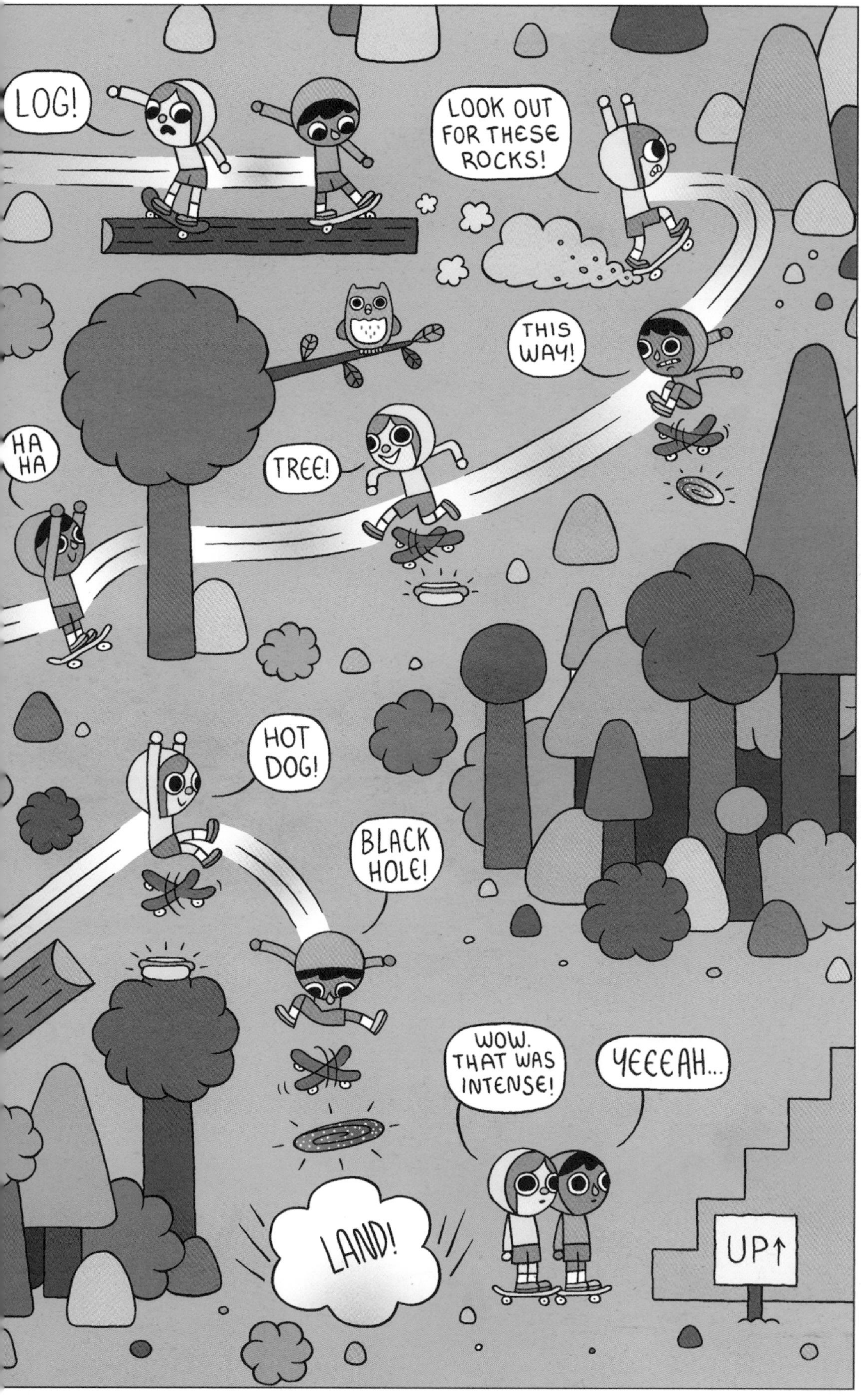
LOG!
LOOK OUT FOR THESE ROCKS!
THIS WAY!
TREE!
HA HA
HOT DOG!
BLACK HOLE!
LAND!
WOW. THAT WAS INTENSE!
YEEEAH...
UP↑

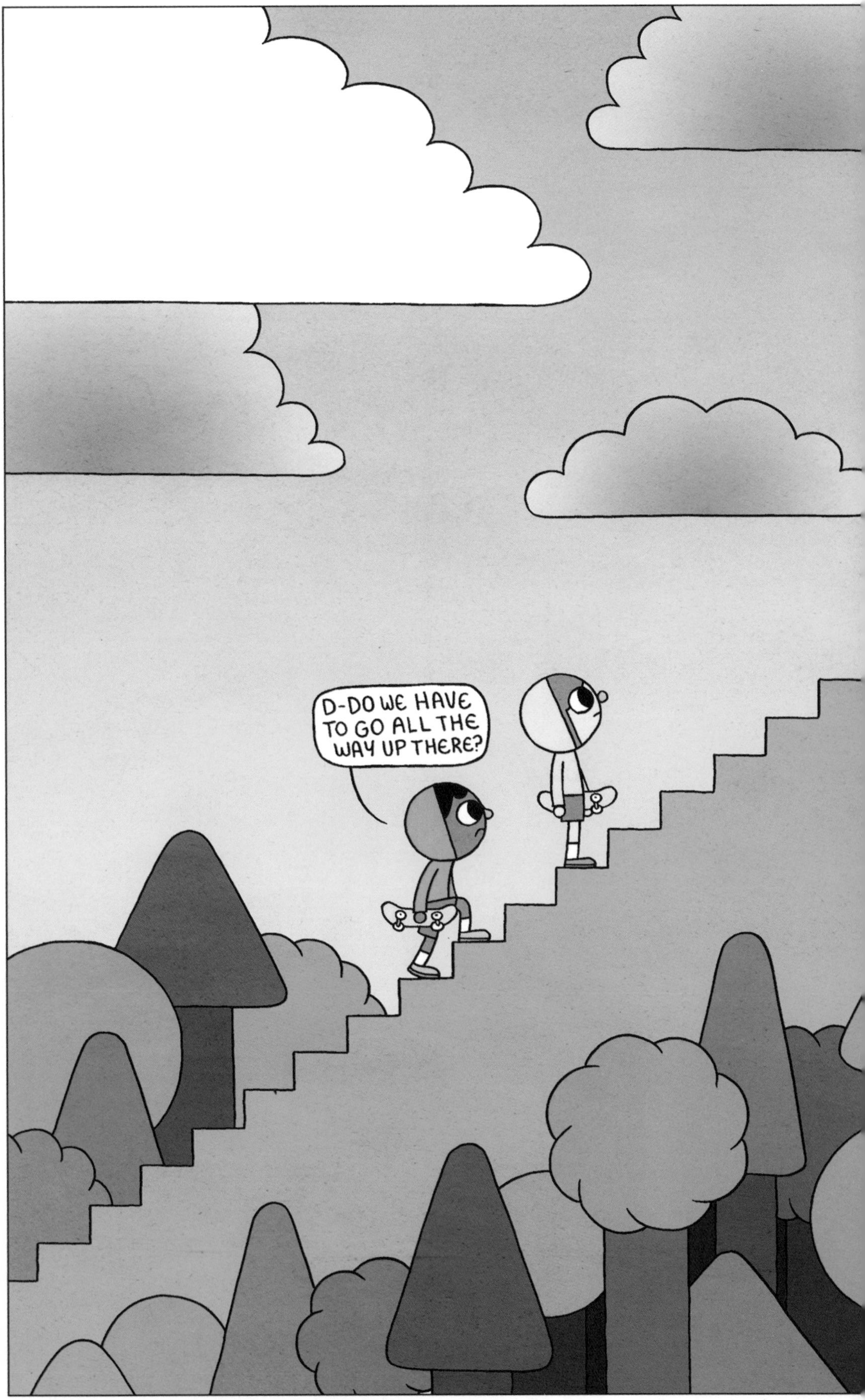
D-DO WE HAVE TO GO ALL THE WAY UP THERE?

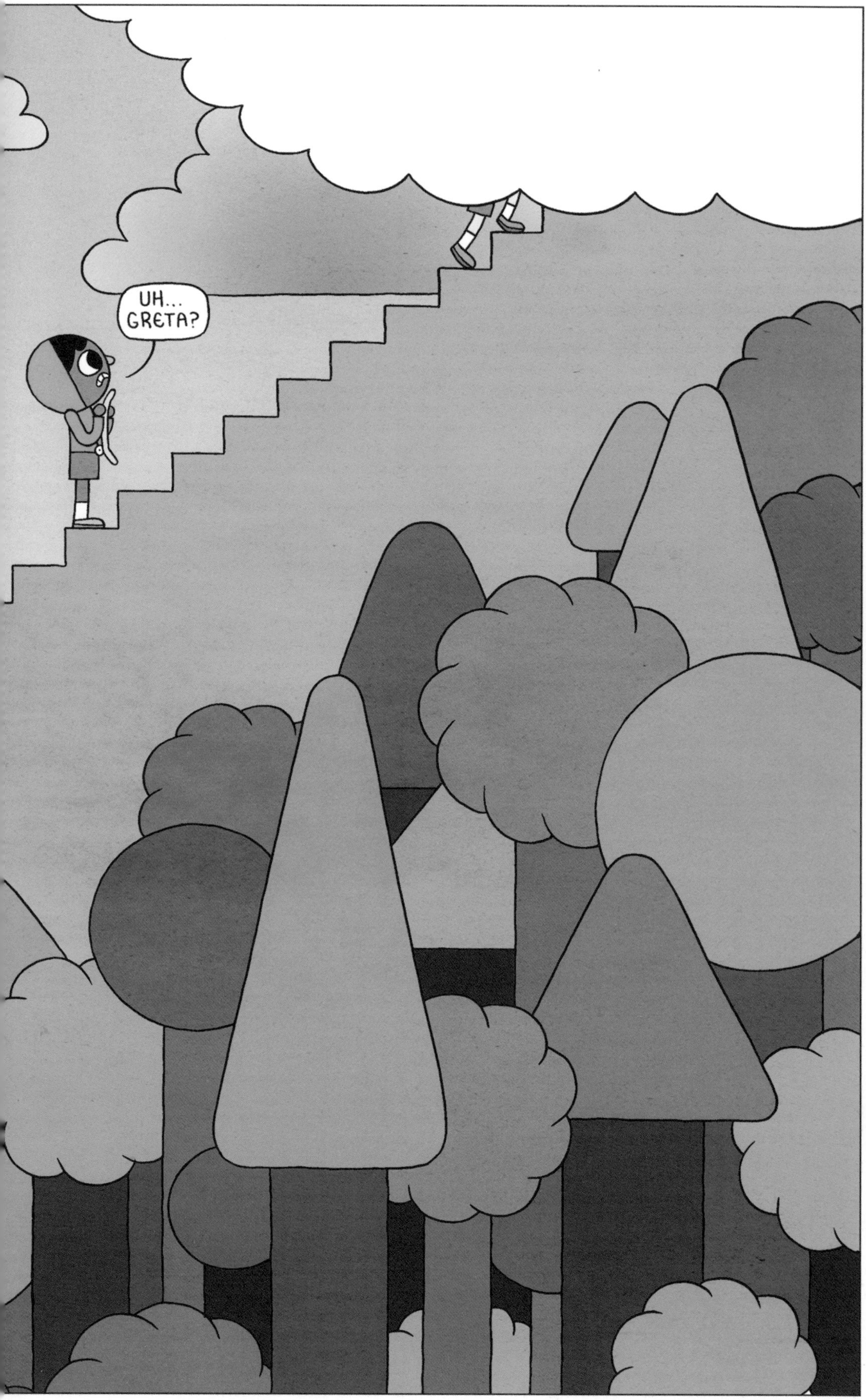
UH... GRETA?

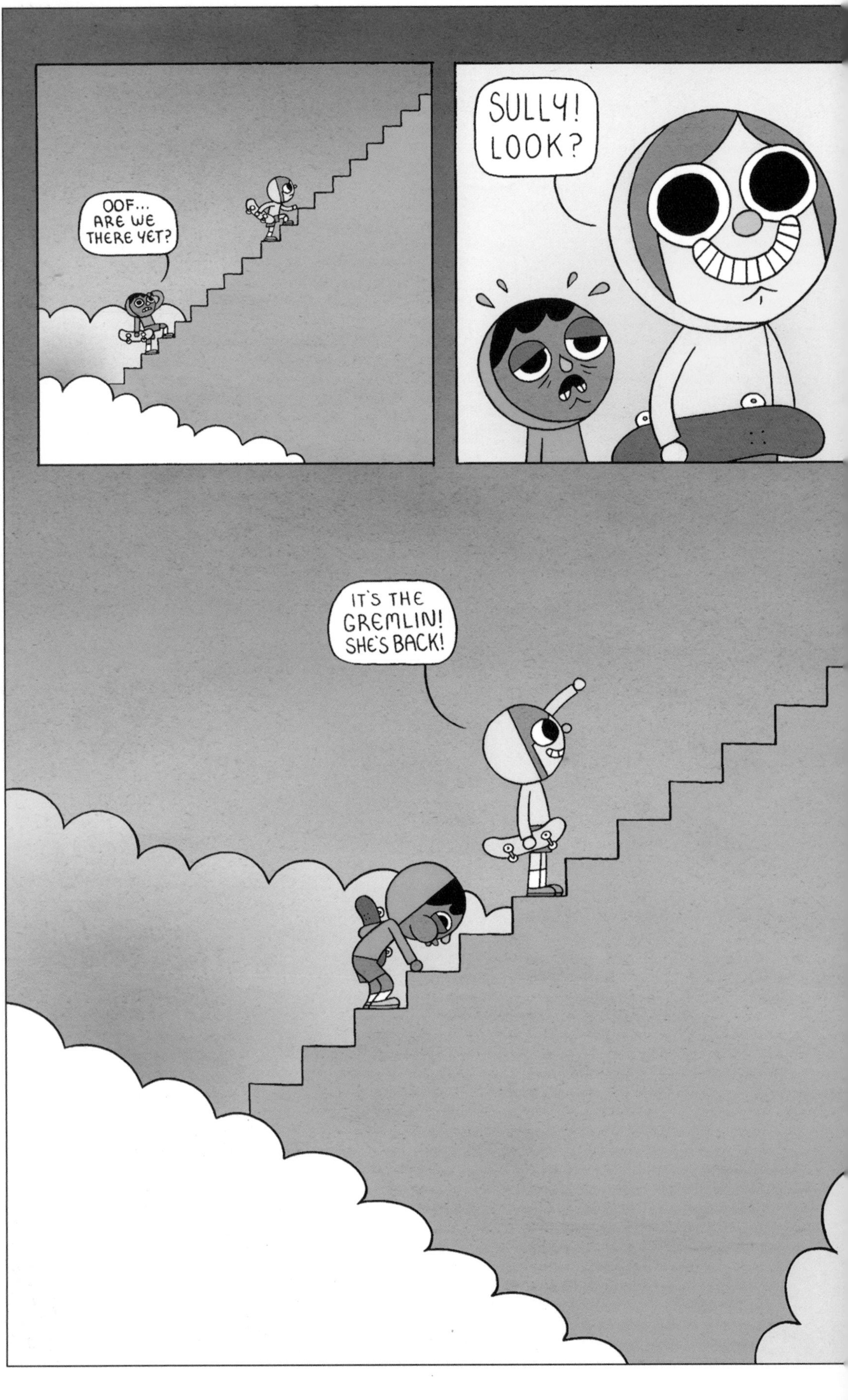
OOF... ARE WE THERE YET?
SULLY! LOOK?
IT'S THE GREMLIN! SHE'S BACK!

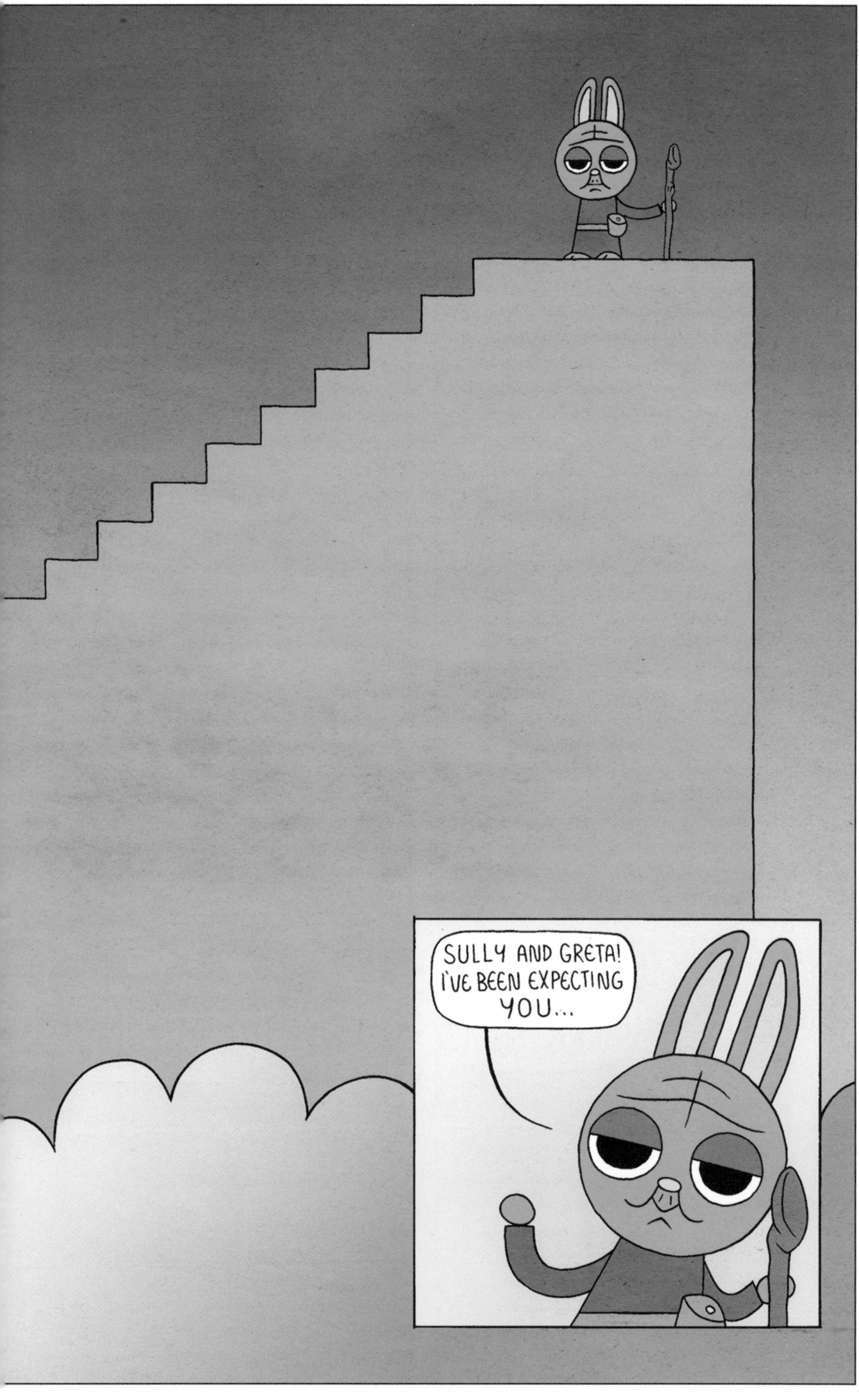
SULLY AND GRETA! I'VE BEEN EXPECTING YOU...

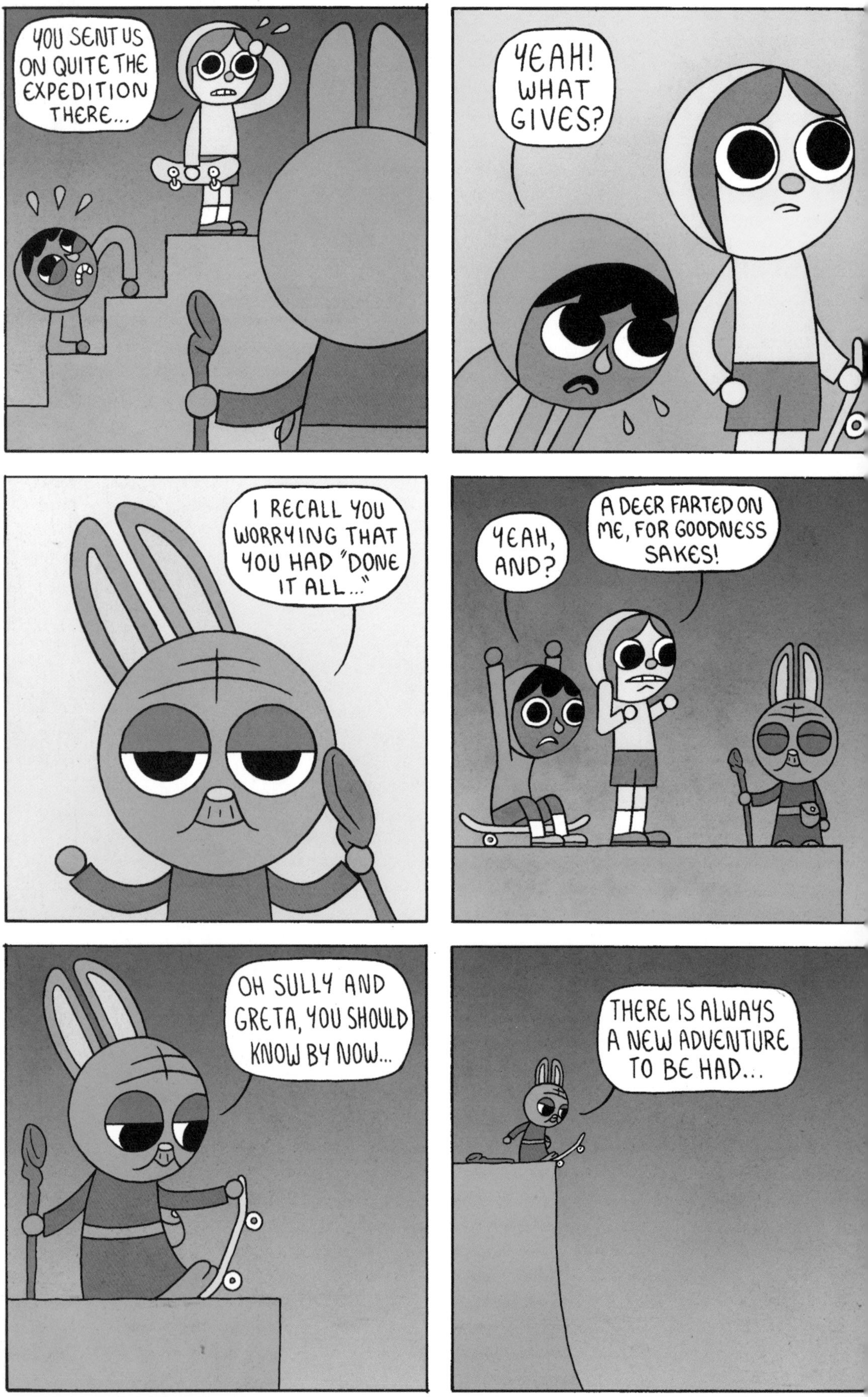
YOU SENT US ON QUITE THE EXPEDITION THERE...
YEAH! WHAT GIVES?
I RECALL YOU WORRYING THAT YOU HAD "DONE IT ALL..."
YEAH, AND?
A DEER FARTED ON ME, FOR GOODNESS SAKES!
OH SULLY AND GRETA, YOU SHOULD KNOW BY NOW...
THERE IS ALWAYS A NEW ADVENTURE TO BE HAD...

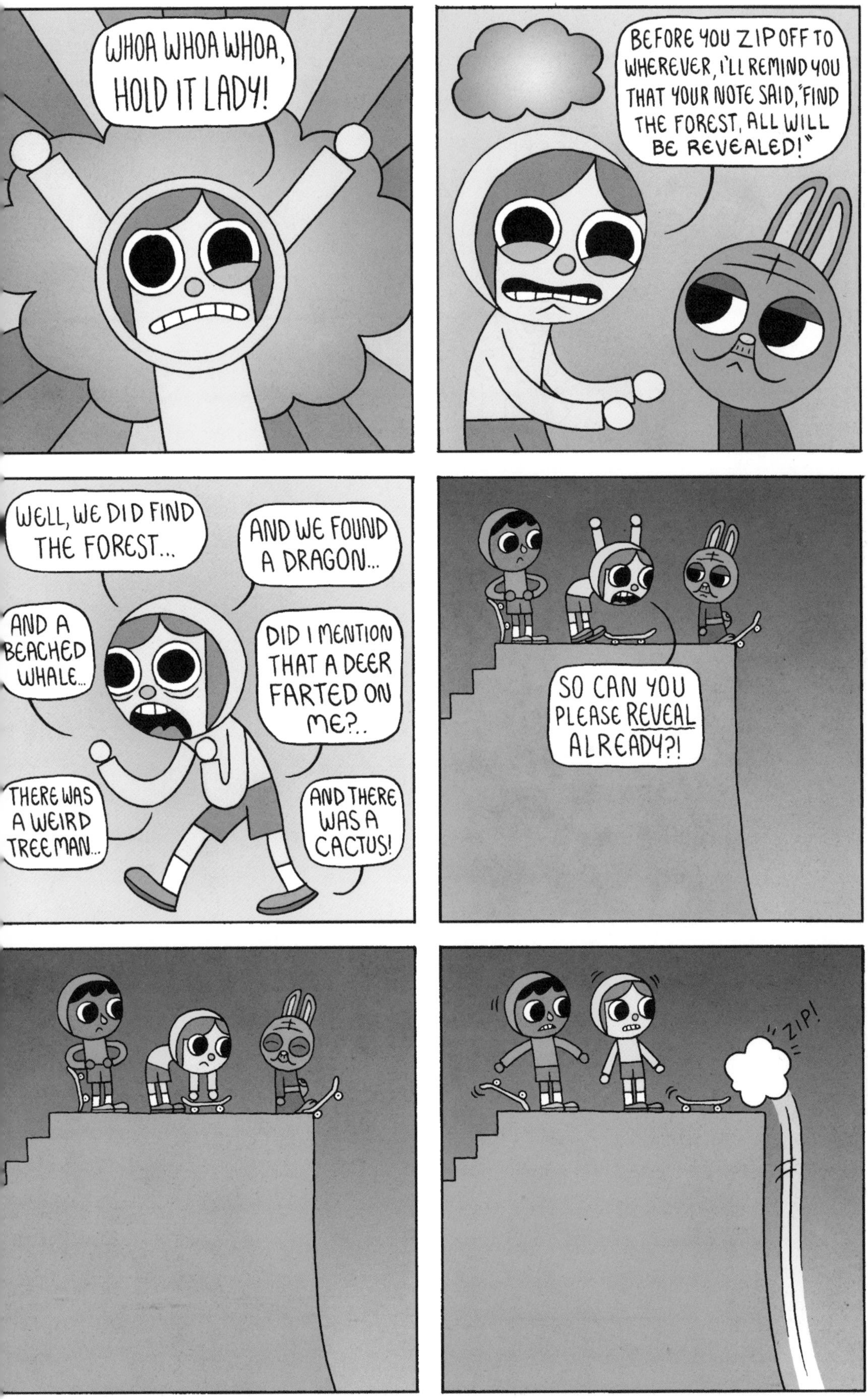
WHOA WHOA WHOA, HOLD IT LADY!
BEFORE YOU ZIP OFF TO WHEREVER, I'LL REMIND YOU THAT YOUR NOTE SAID, "FIND THE FOREST, ALL WILL BE REVEALED!"
WELL, WE DID FIND THE FOREST...
AND WE FOUND A DRAGON...
AND A BEACHED WHALE...
DID I MENTION THAT A DEER FARTED ON ME?..
THERE WAS A WEIRD TREE MAN...
AND THERE WAS A CACTUS!
SO CAN YOU PLEASE REVEAL ALREADY?!
ZIP!

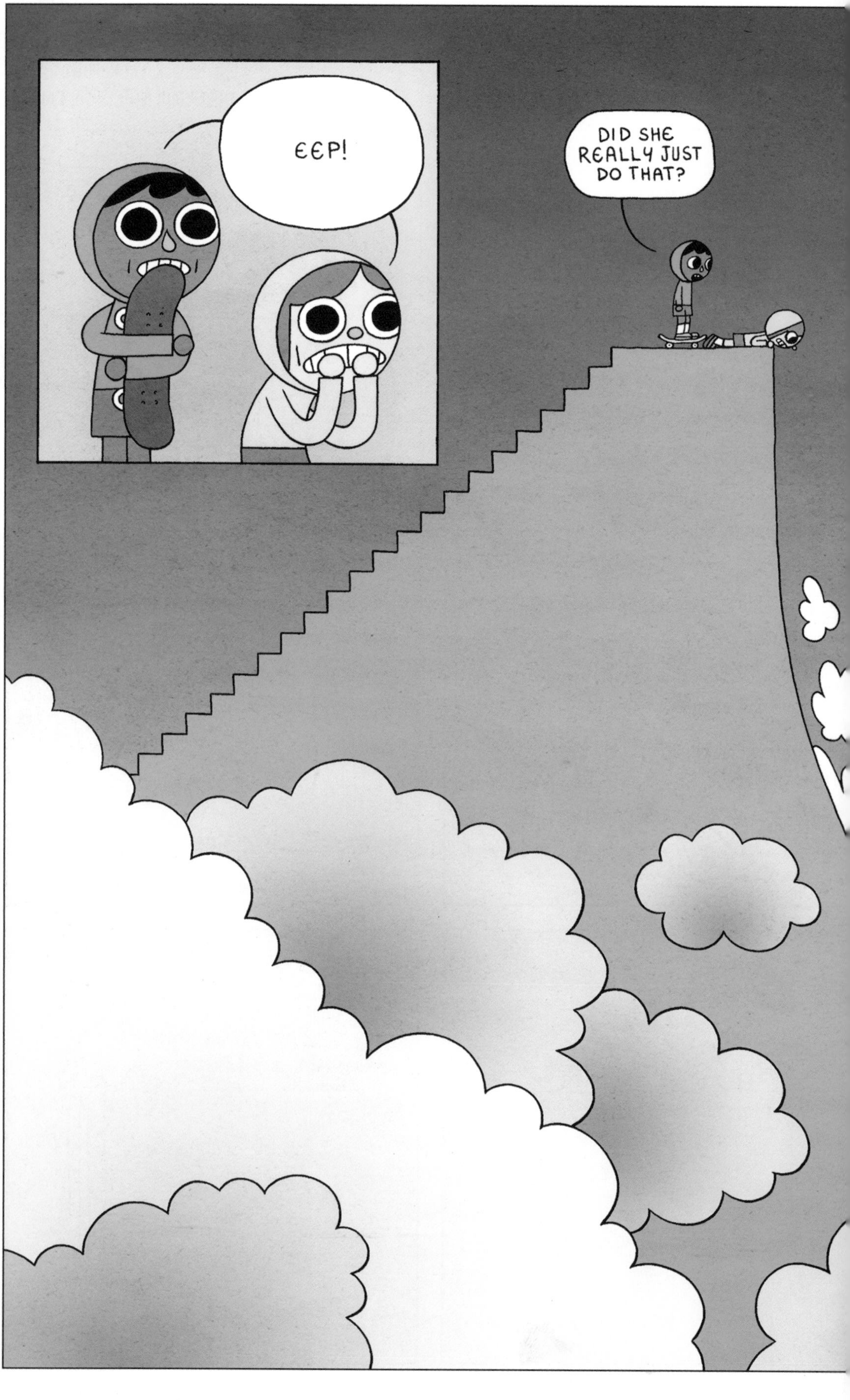
EEP!
DID SHE REALLY JUST DO THAT?

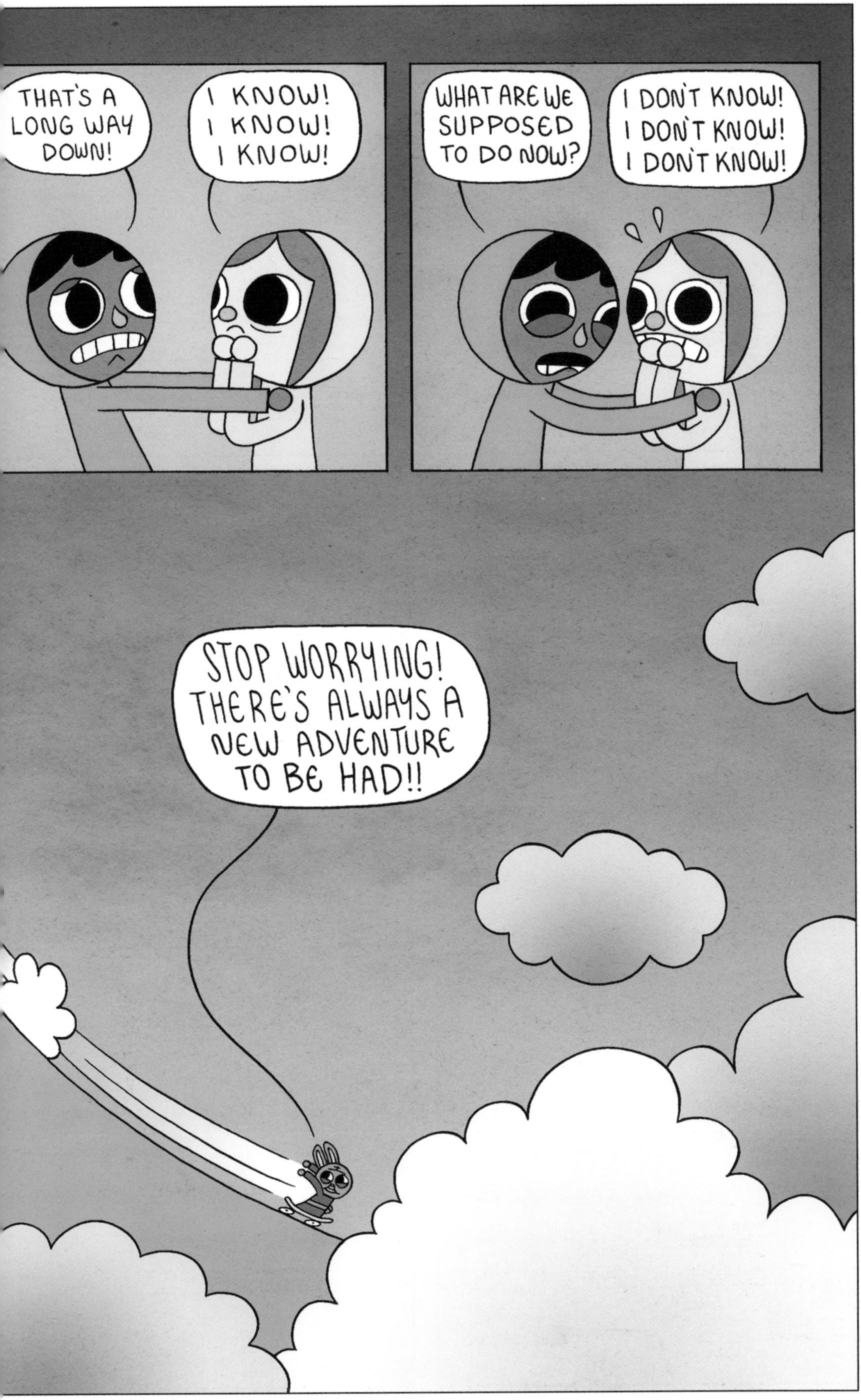
THAT'S A LONG WAY DOWN!
I KNOW! I KNOW! I KNOW!
WHAT ARE WE SUPPOSED TO DO NOW?
I DON'T KNOW! I DON'T KNOW! I DON'T KNOW!
STOP WORRYING! THERE'S ALWAYS A NEW ADVENTURE TO BE HAD!!

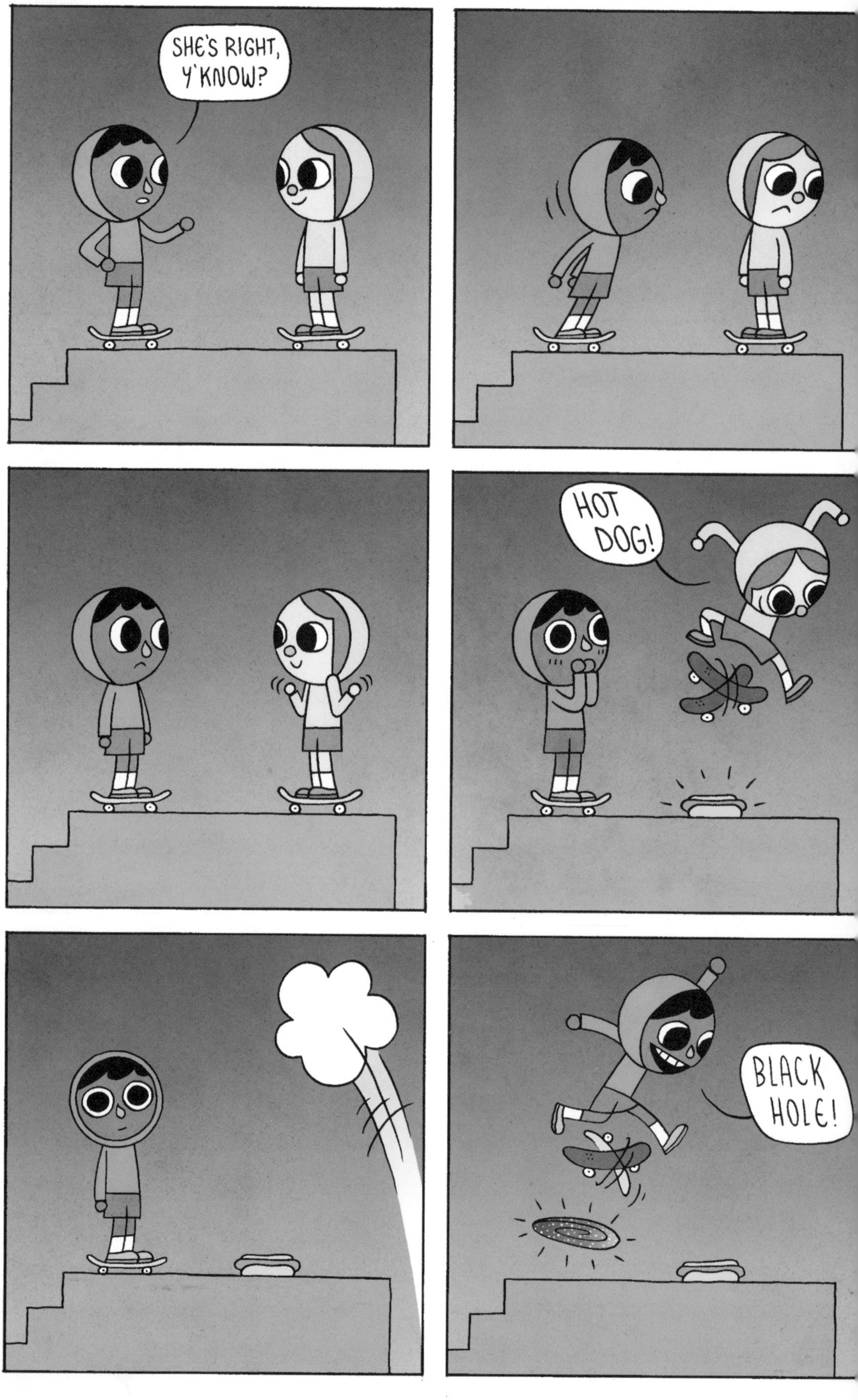
SHE'S RIGHT, Y'KNOW?
HOT DOG!
BLACK HOLE!

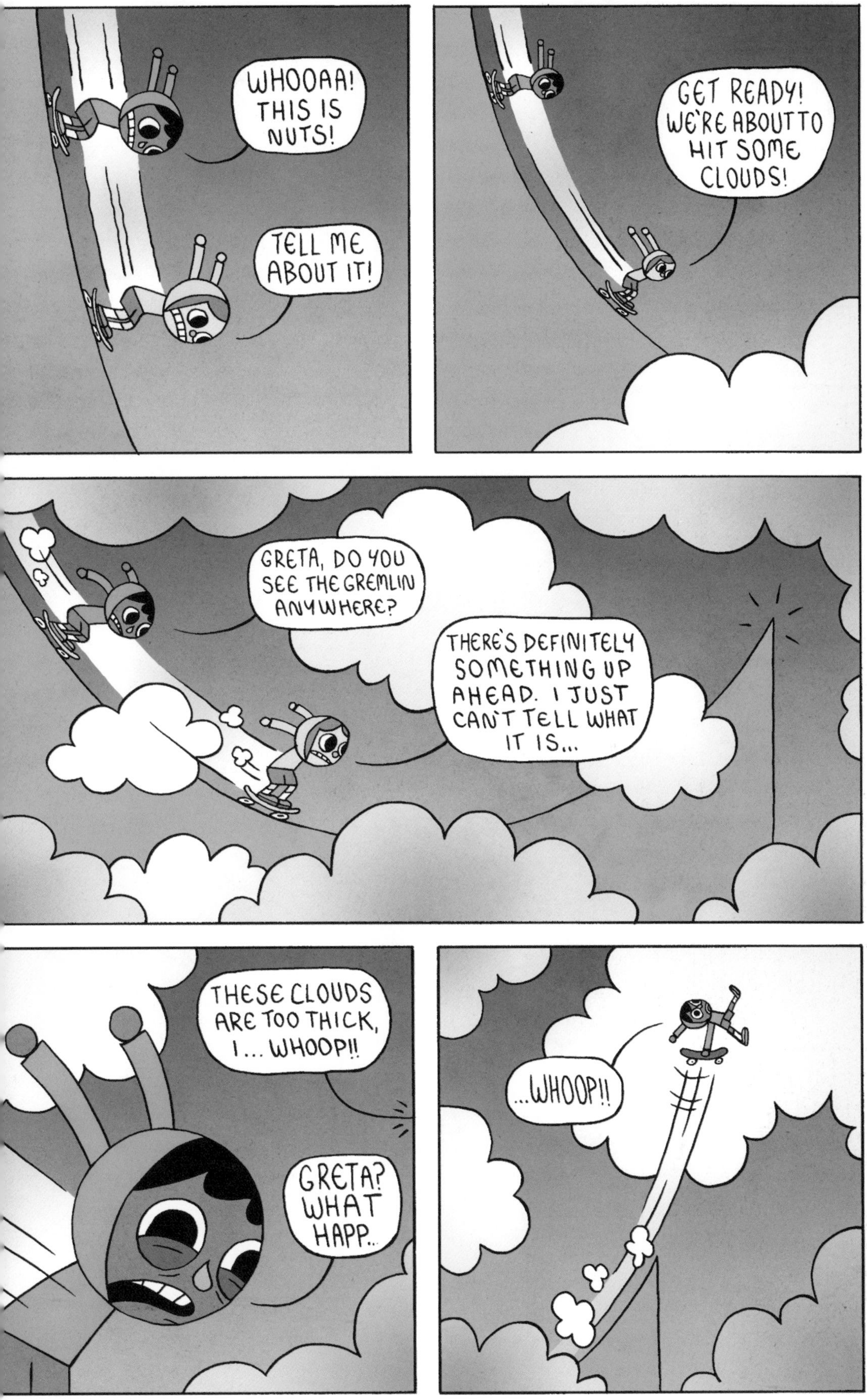
WHOOAA! THIS IS NUTS!
TELL ME ABOUT IT!
GET READY! WE'RE ABOUT TO HIT SOME CLOUDS!
GRETA, DO YOU SEE THE GREMLIN ANYWHERE?
THERE'S DEFINITELY SOMETHING UP AHEAD. I JUST CAN'T TELL WHAT IT IS...
THESE CLOUDS ARE TOO THICK, I... WHOOP!!
GRETA? WHAT HAPP...
...WHOOP!!

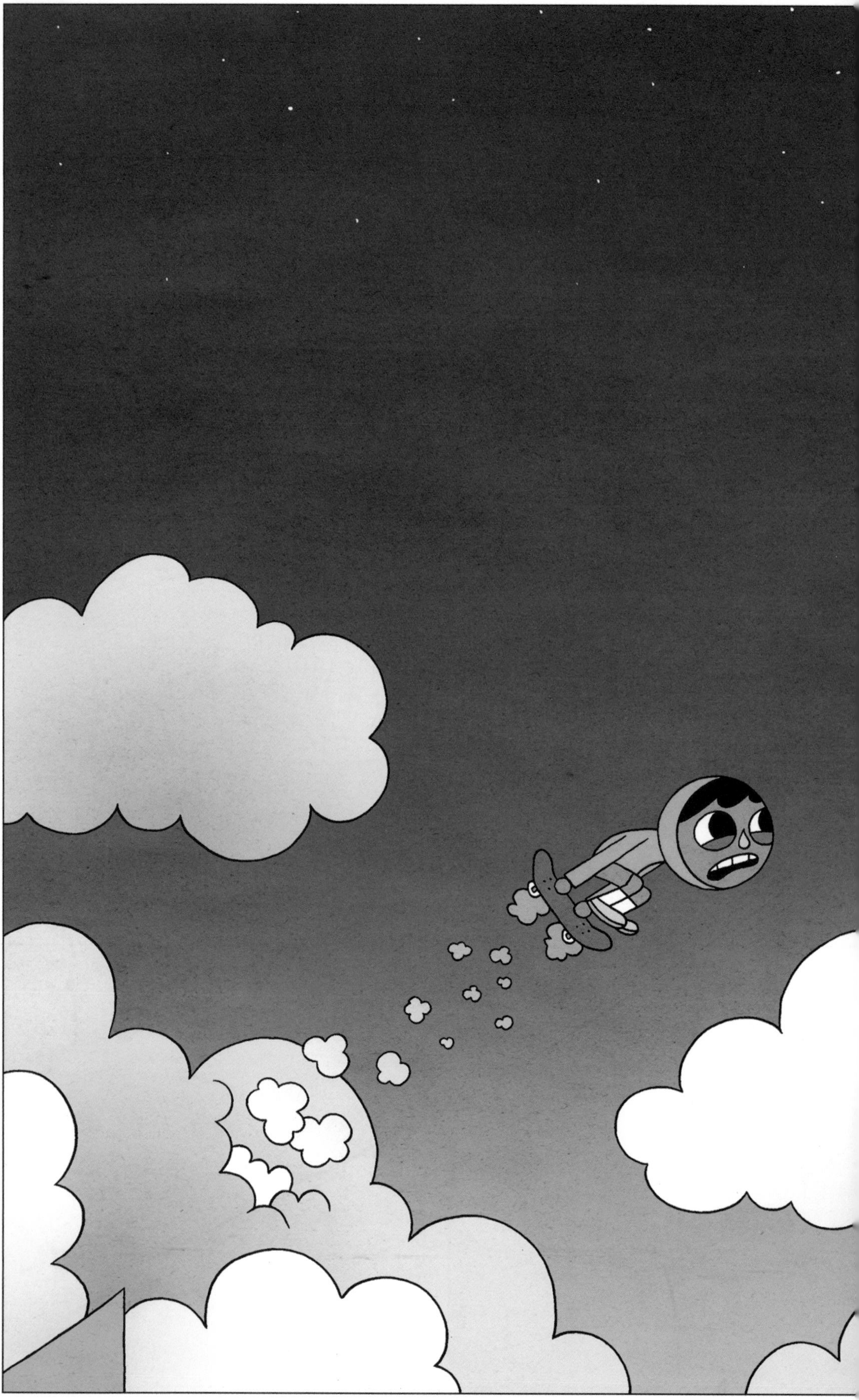

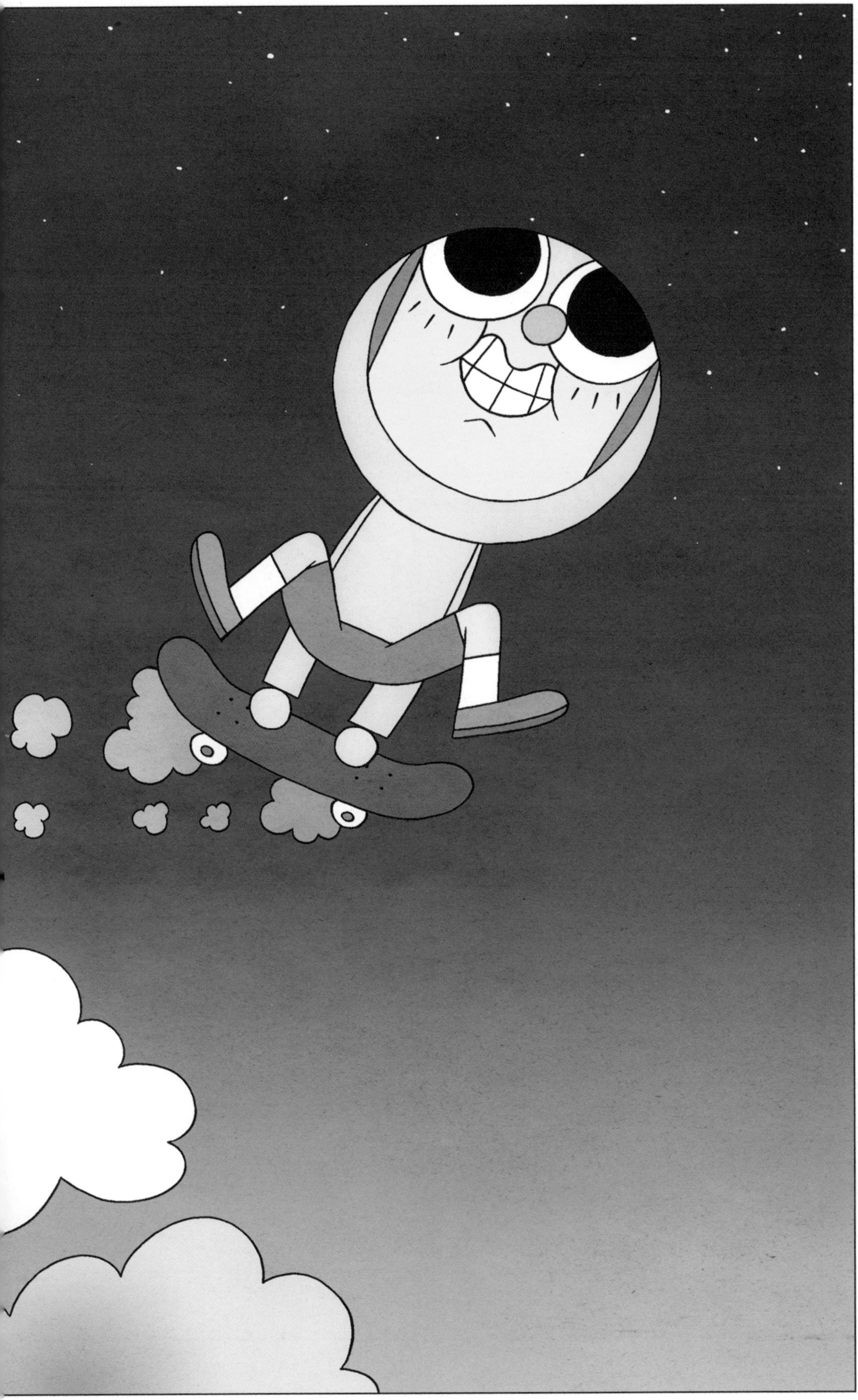

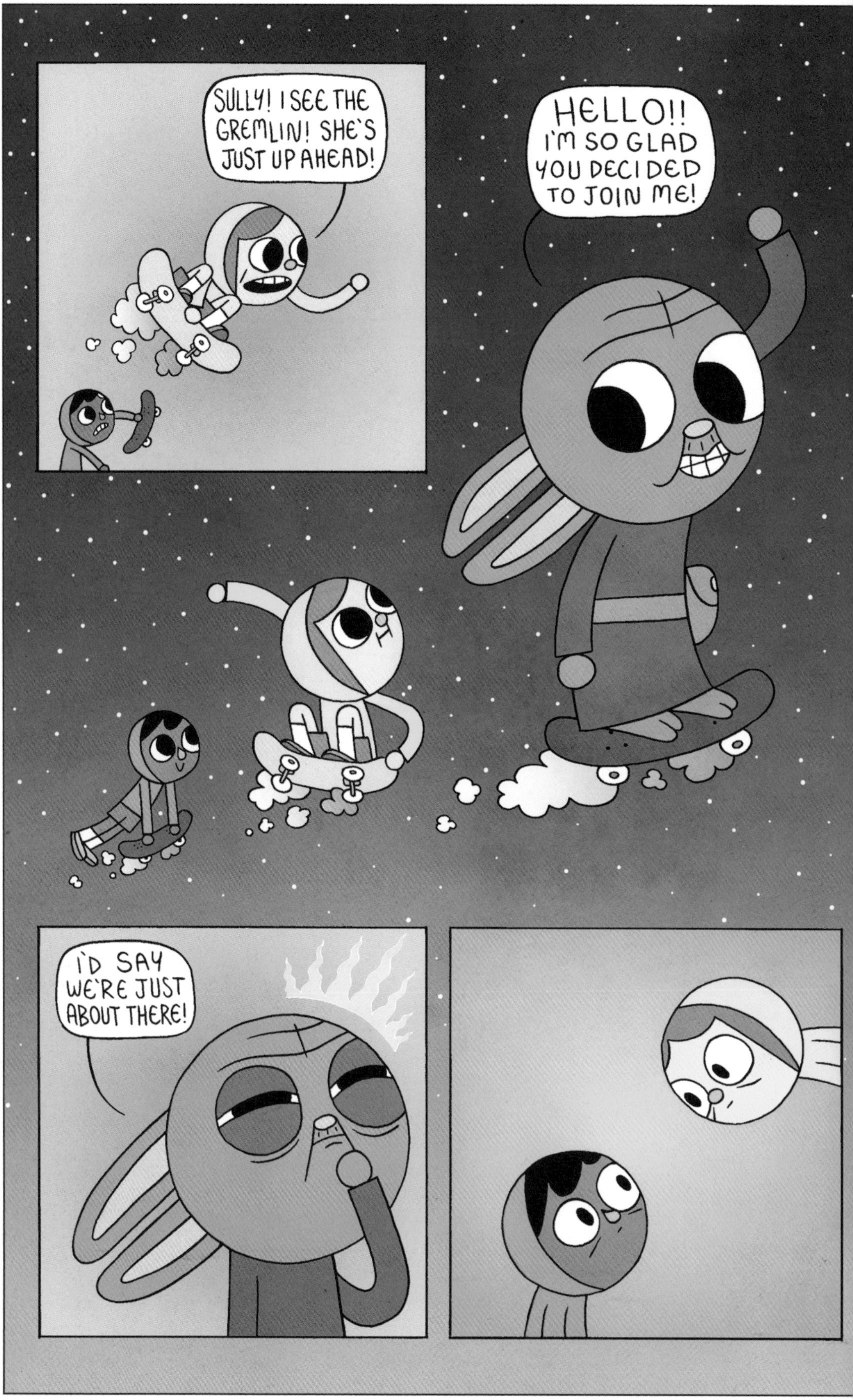
SULLY! I SEE THE GREMLIN! SHE'S JUST UP AHEAD!
HELLO!! I'M SO GLAD YOU DECIDED TO JOIN ME!
I'D SAY WE'RE JUST ABOUT THERE!

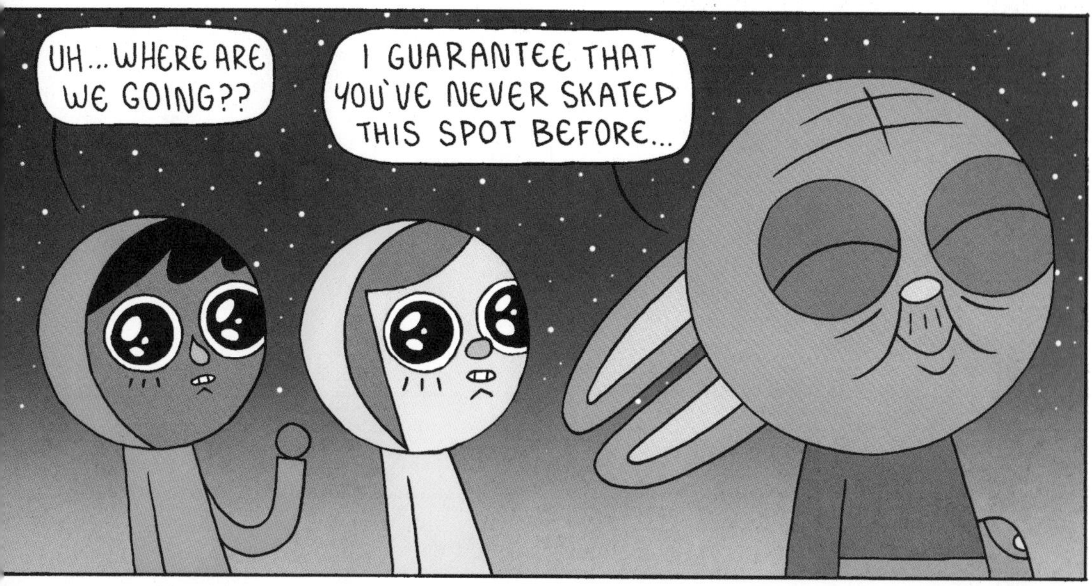
UH... WHERE ARE WE GOING??
I GUARANTEE THAT YOU'VE NEVER SKATED THIS SPOT BEFORE...

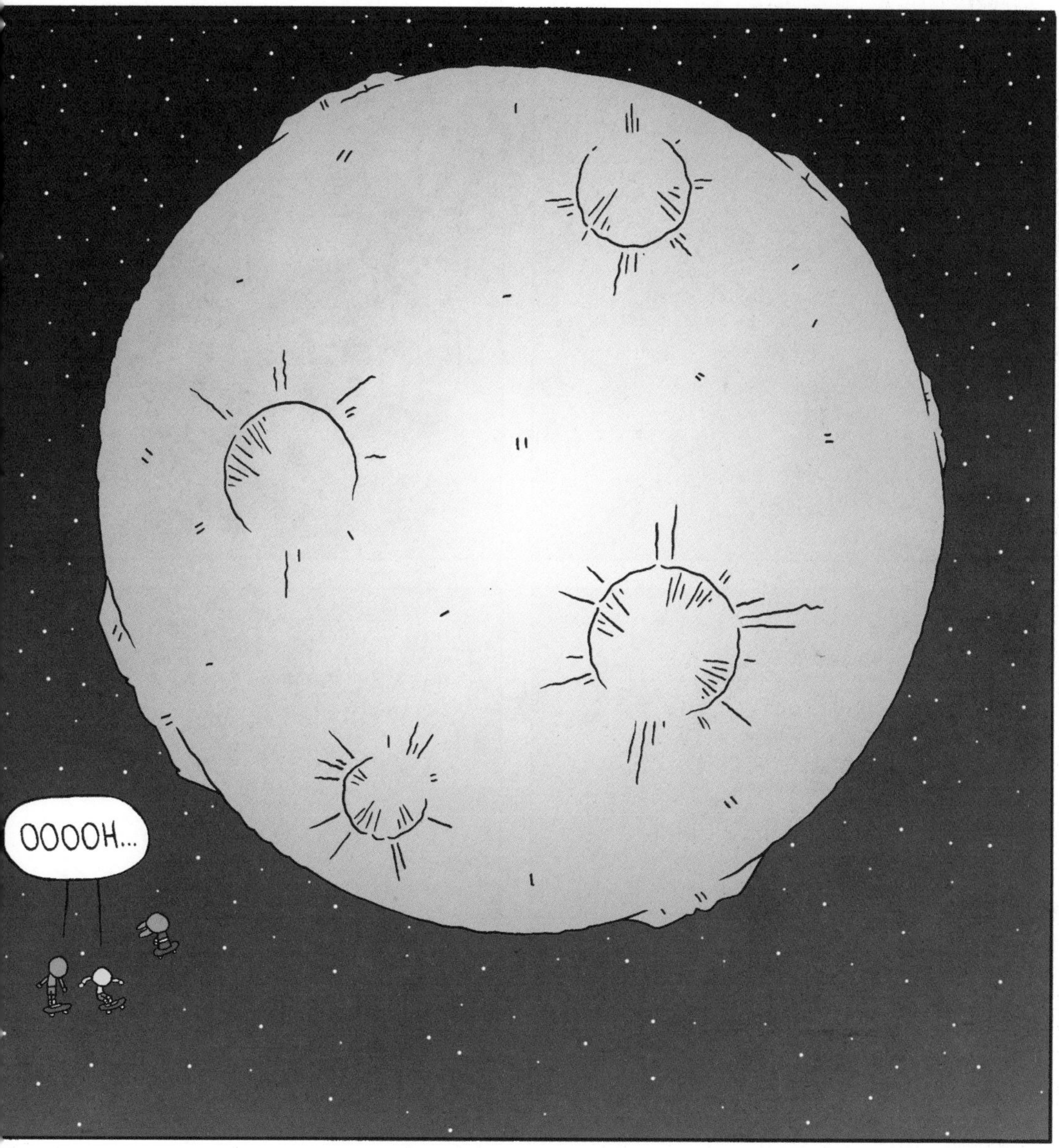
OOOOH...

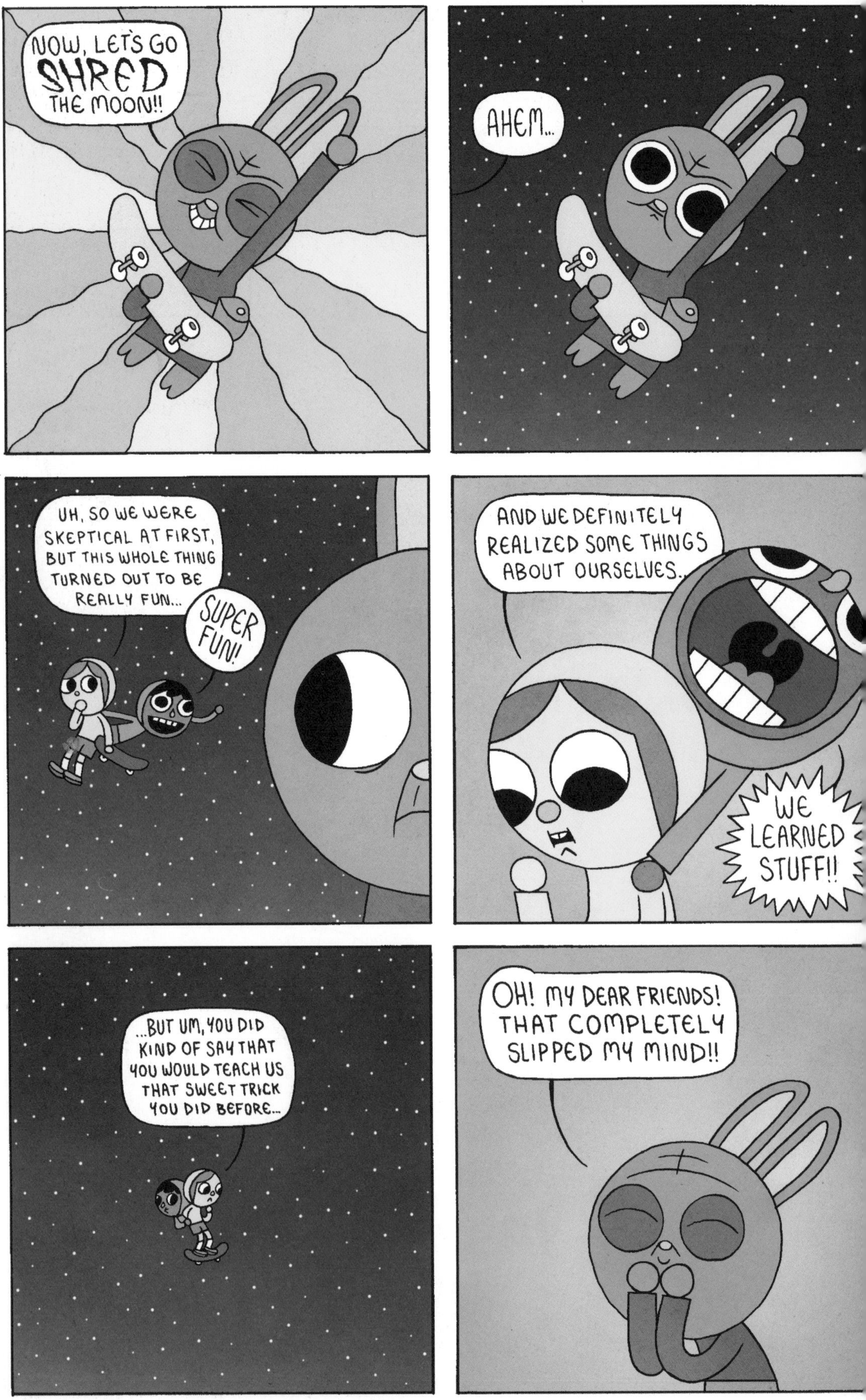
NOW, LET'S GO SHRED THE MOON!!
AHEM...
UH, SO WE WERE SKEPTICAL AT FIRST, BUT THIS WHOLE THING TURNED OUT TO BE REALLY FUN...
SUPER FUN!
AND WE DEFINITELY REALIZED SOME THINGS ABOUT OURSELVES...
WE LEARNED STUFF!!
...BUT UM, YOU DID KIND OF SAY THAT YOU WOULD TEACH US THAT SWEET TRICK YOU DID BEFORE...
OH! MY DEAR FRIENDS! THAT COMPLETELY SLIPPED MY MIND!!

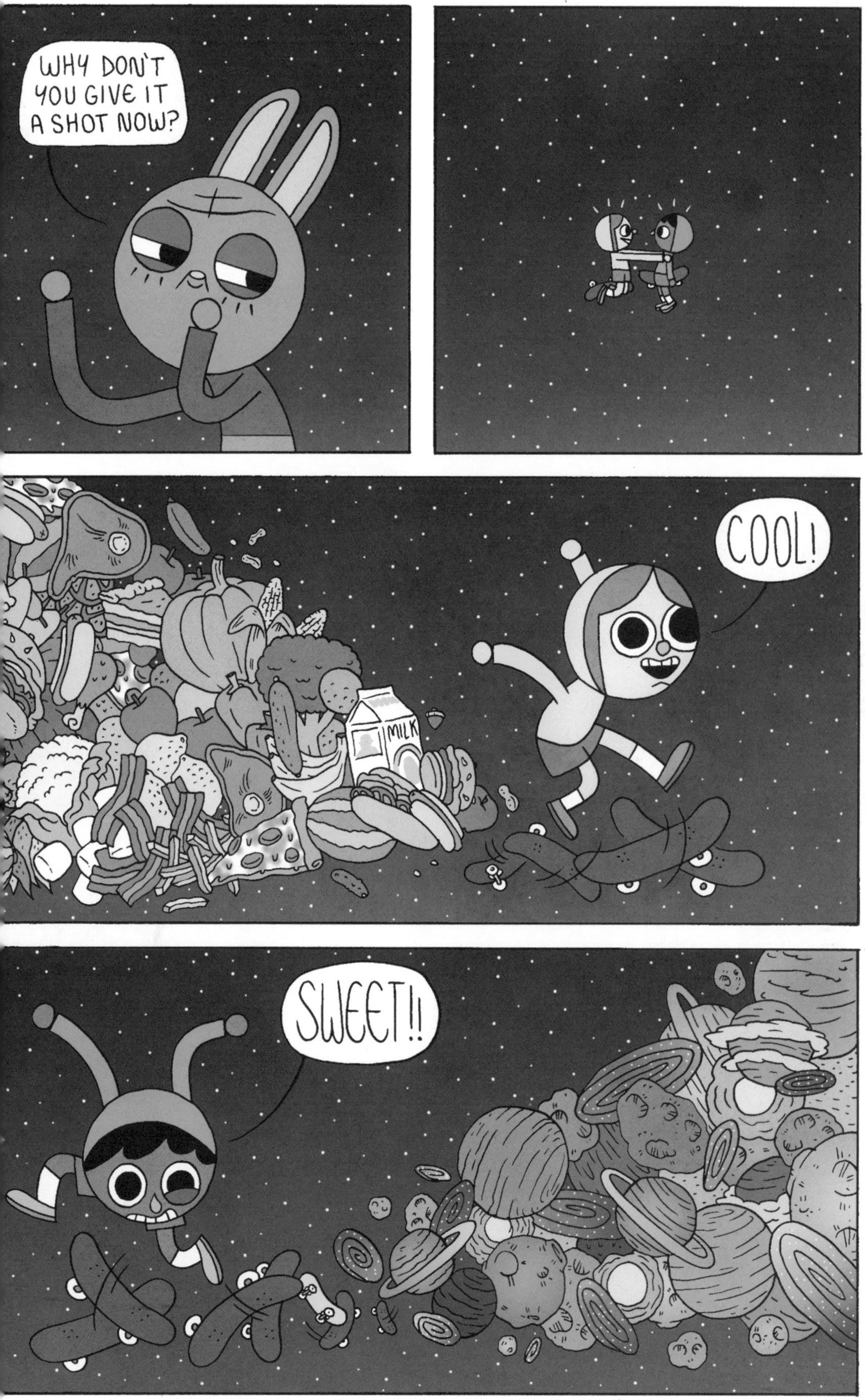
WHY DON'T YOU GIVE IT A SHOT NOW?
COOL!
MILK
SWEET!!

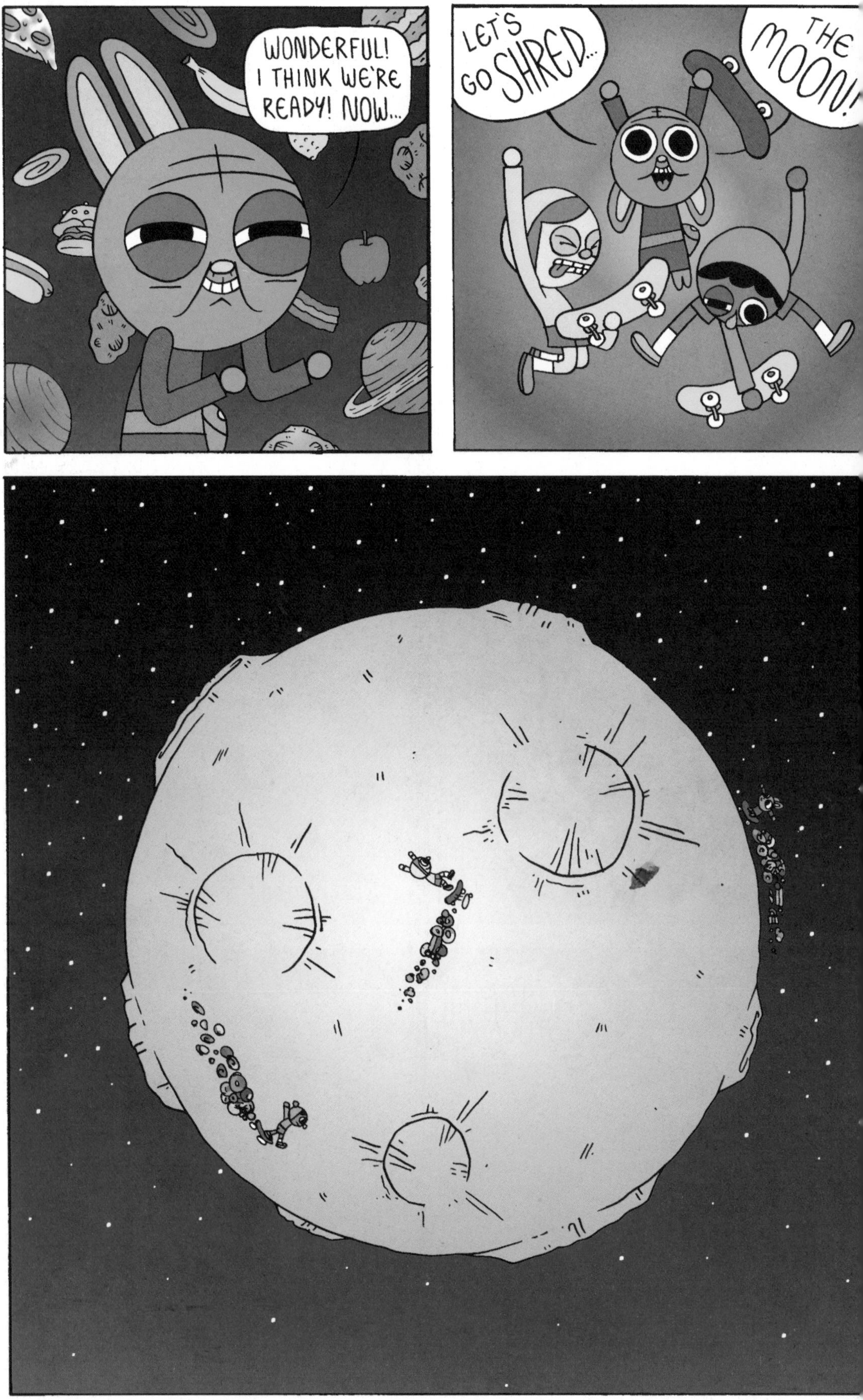
WONDERFUL! I THINK WE'RE READY! NOW...
LET'S GO SHRED...
THE MOON!

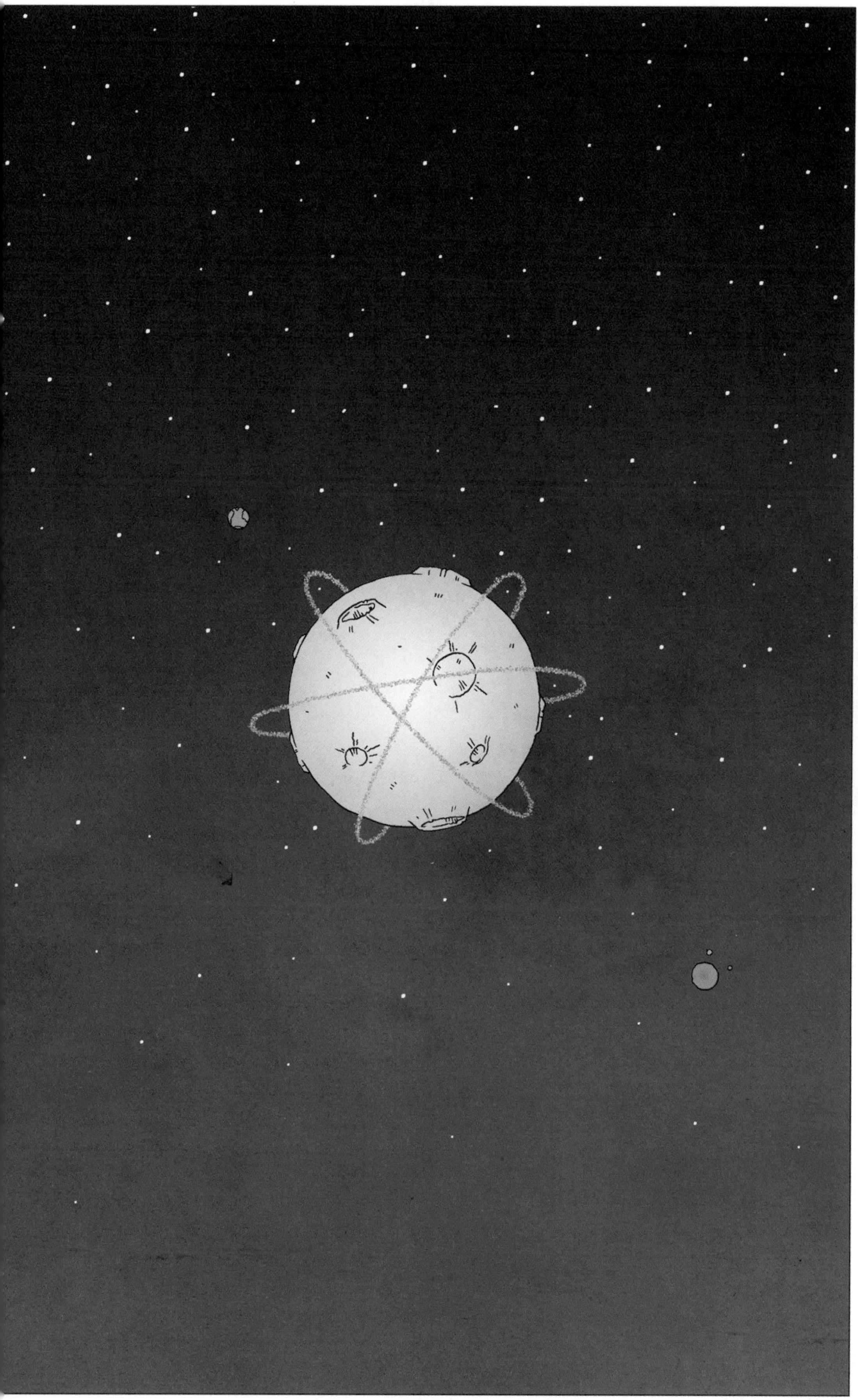

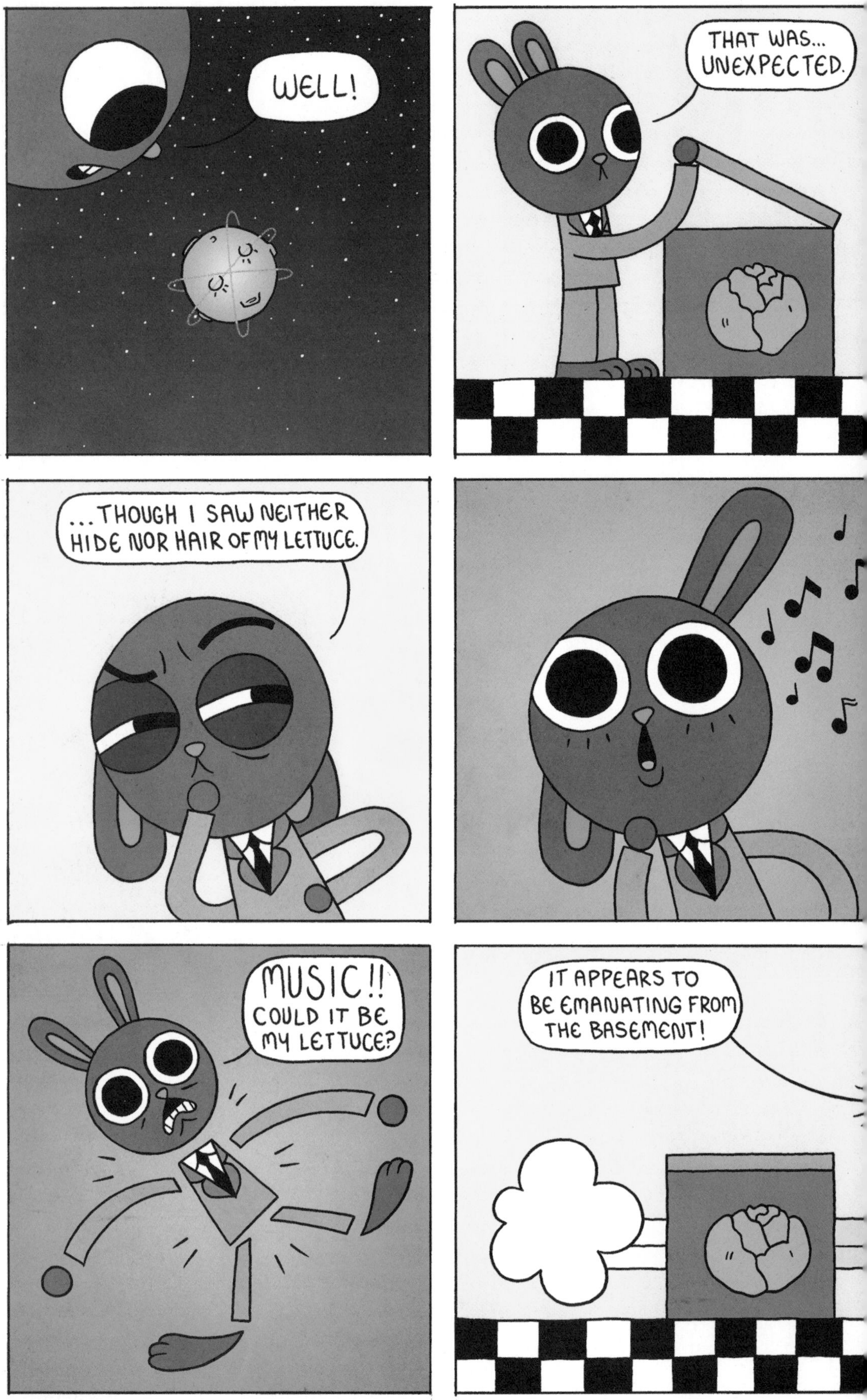
WELL!
THAT WAS... UNEXPECTED.
...THOUGH I SAW NEITHER HIDE NOR HAIR OF MY LETTUCE.
MUSIC!! COULD IT BE MY LETTUCE?
IT APPEARS TO BE EMANATING FROM THE BASEMENT!

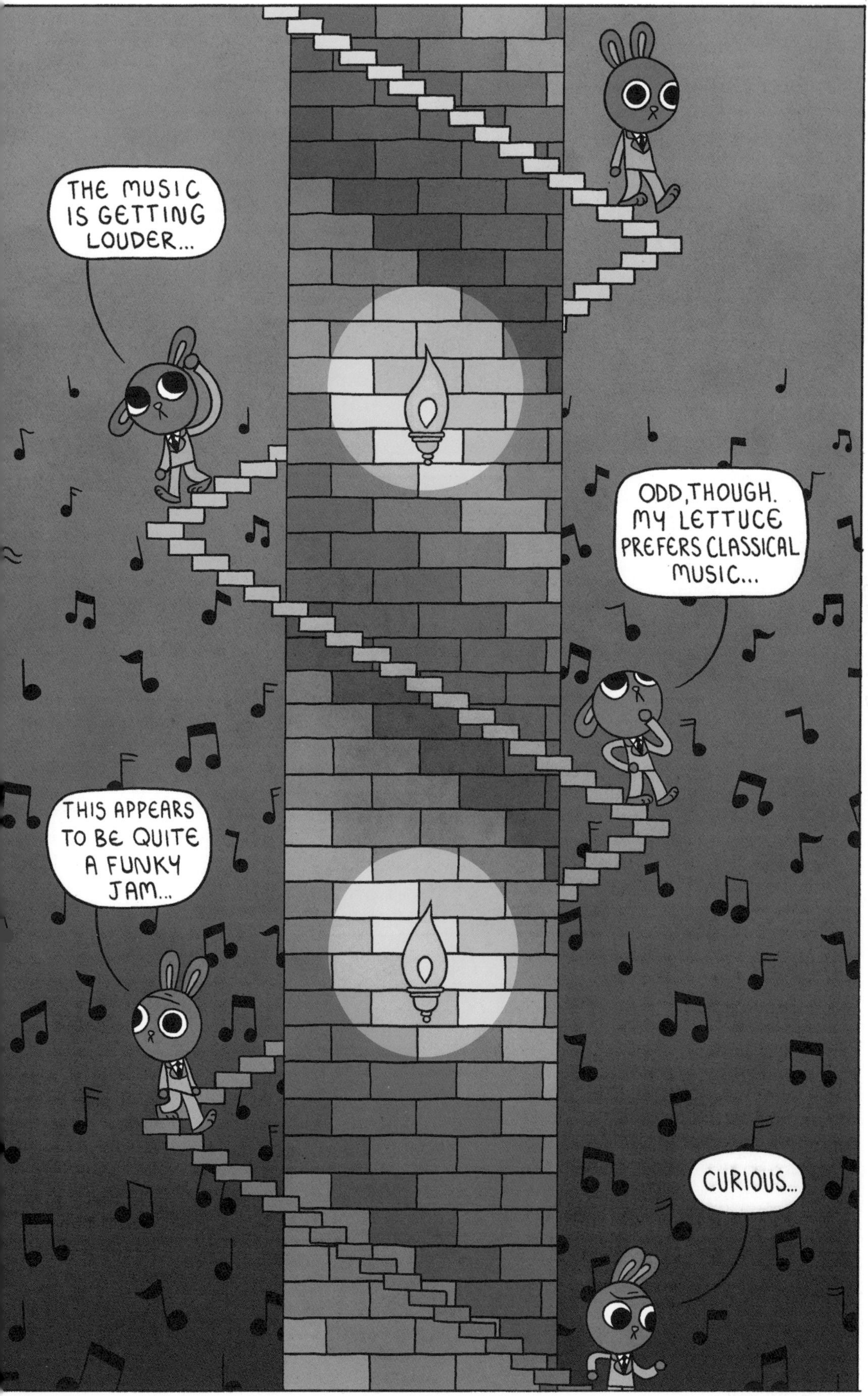
THE MUSIC IS GETTING LOUDER...
ODD, THOUGH. MY LETTUCE PREFERS CLASSICAL MUSIC...
THIS APPEARS TO BE QUITE A FUNKY JAM...
CURIOUS...

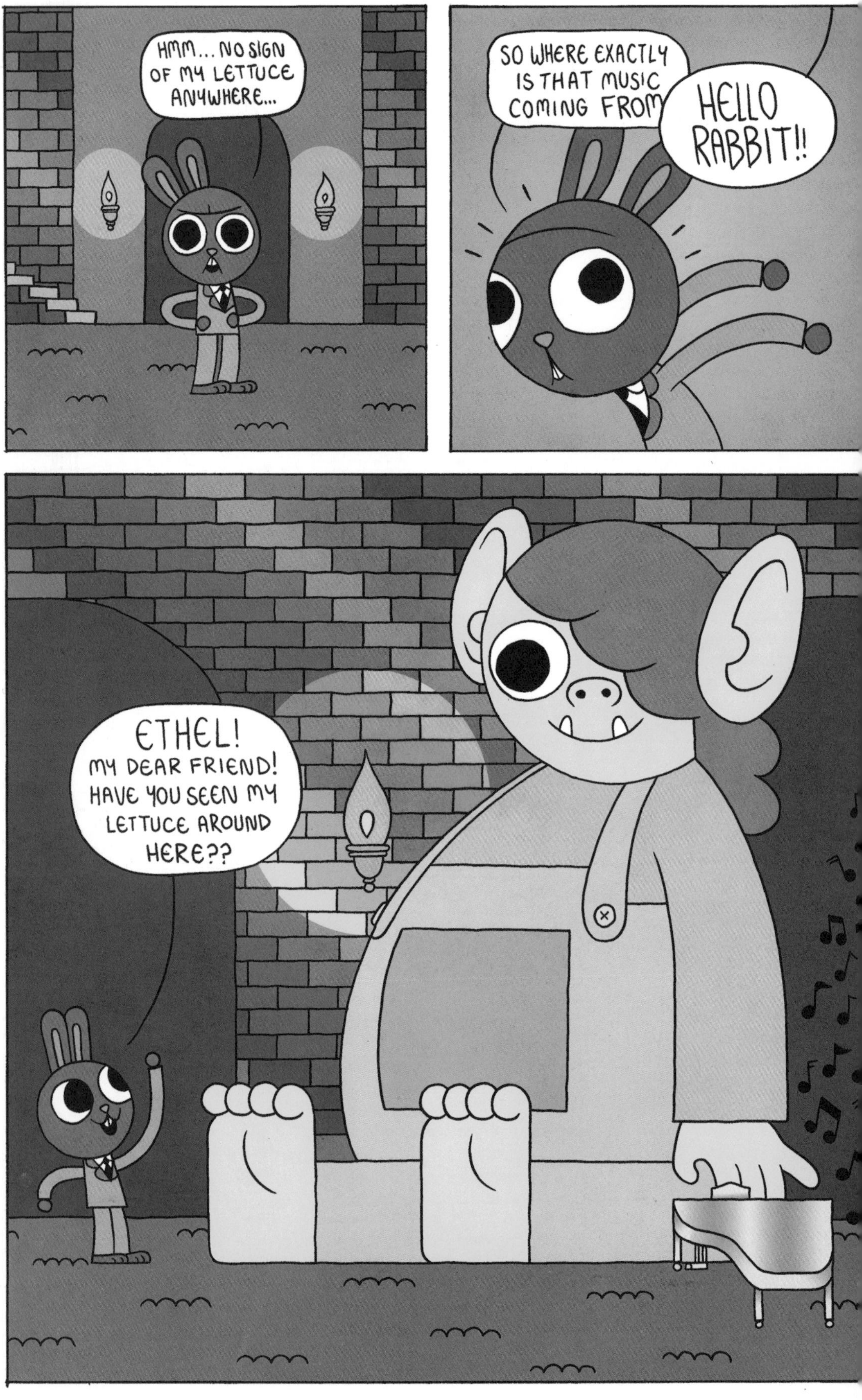

HMM... NO SIGN OF MY LETTUCE ANYWHERE...
SO WHERE EXACTLY IS THAT MUSIC COMING FROM
HELLO RABBIT!!
ETHEL! MY DEAR FRIEND! HAVE YOU SEEN MY LETTUCE AROUND HERE??

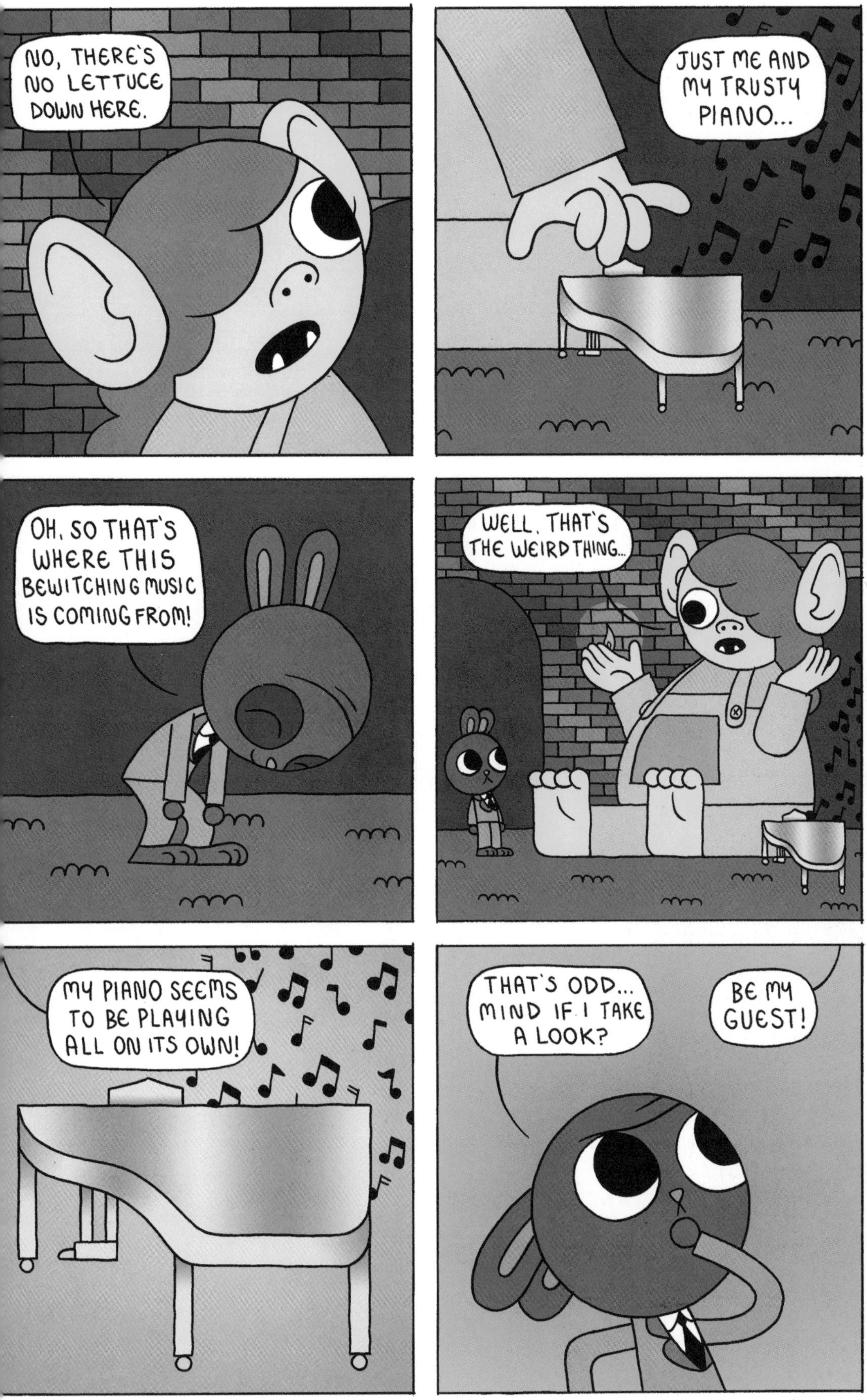
NO, THERE'S NO LETTUCE DOWN HERE.
JUST ME AND MY TRUSTY PIANO...
OH, SO THAT'S WHERE THIS BEWITCHING MUSIC IS COMING FROM!
WELL, THAT'S THE WEIRD THING...
MY PIANO SEEMS TO BE PLAYING ALL ON ITS OWN!
THAT'S ODD... MIND IF I TAKE A LOOK?
BE MY GUEST!

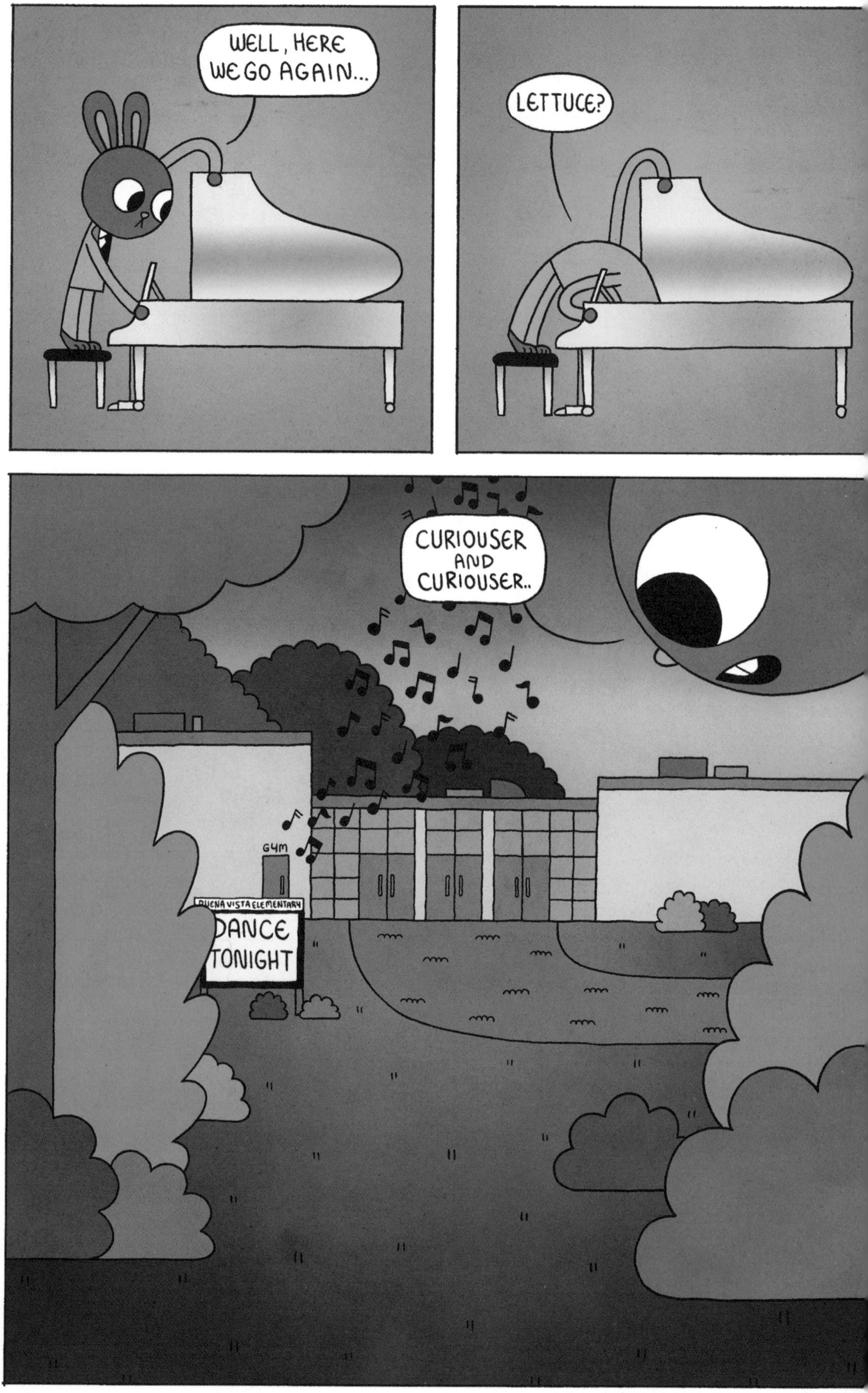

WELL, HERE WE GO AGAIN...
LETTUCE?
CURIOUSER AND CURIOUSER..
GYM
BUENA VISTA ELEMENTARY
DANCE TONIGHT

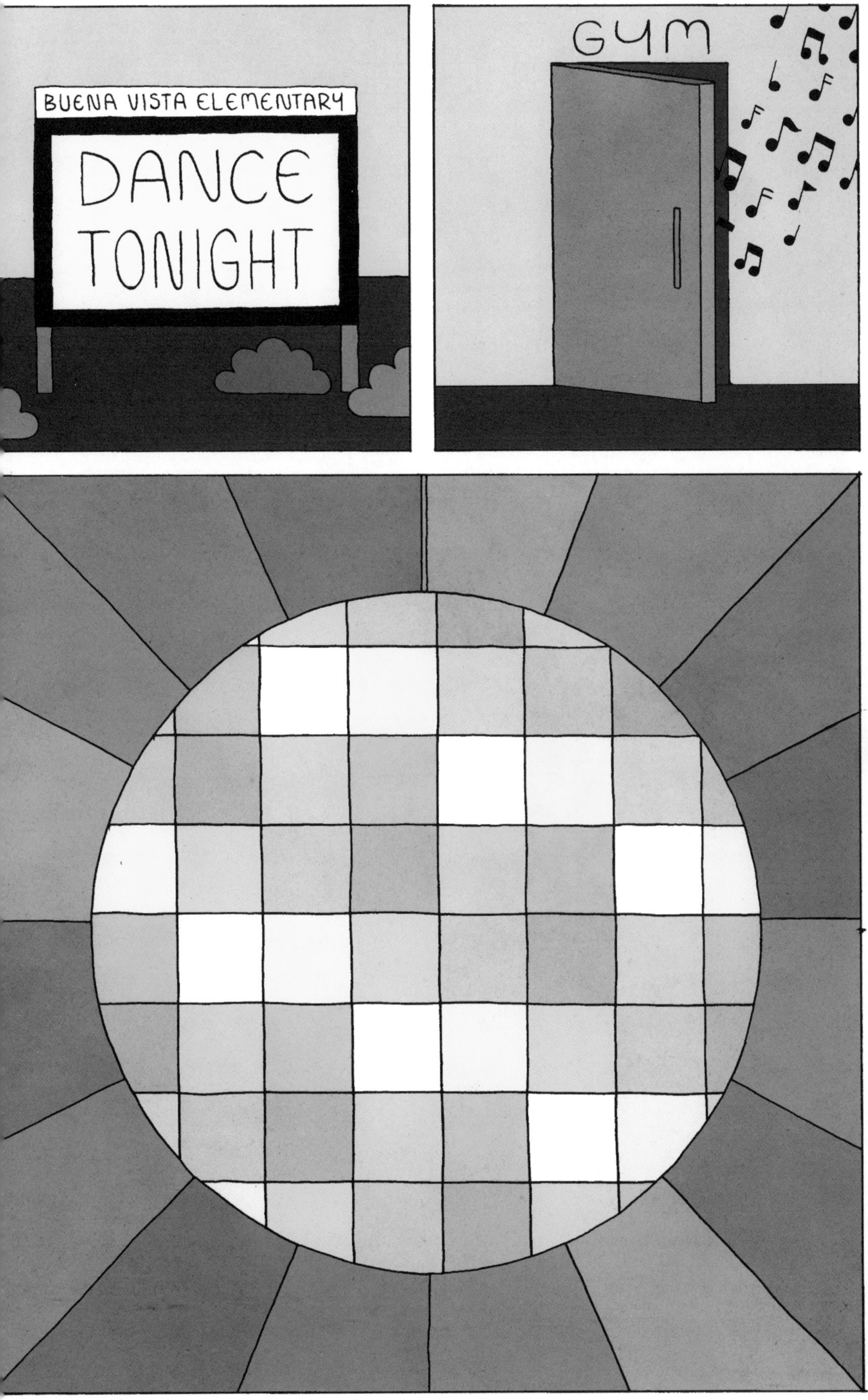
BUENA VISTA ELEMENTARY
DANCE TONIGHT
GYM

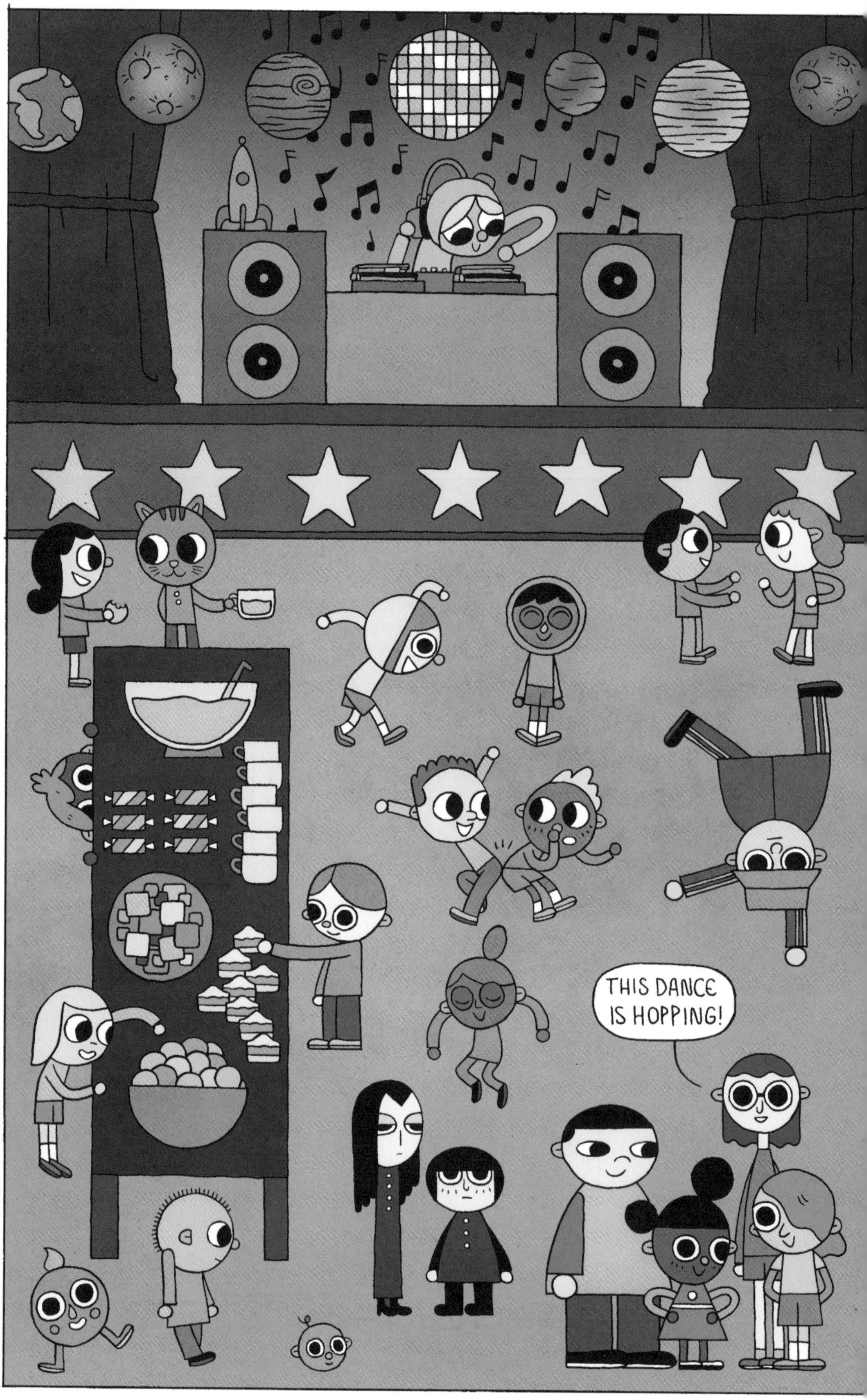
THIS DANCE IS HOPPING!

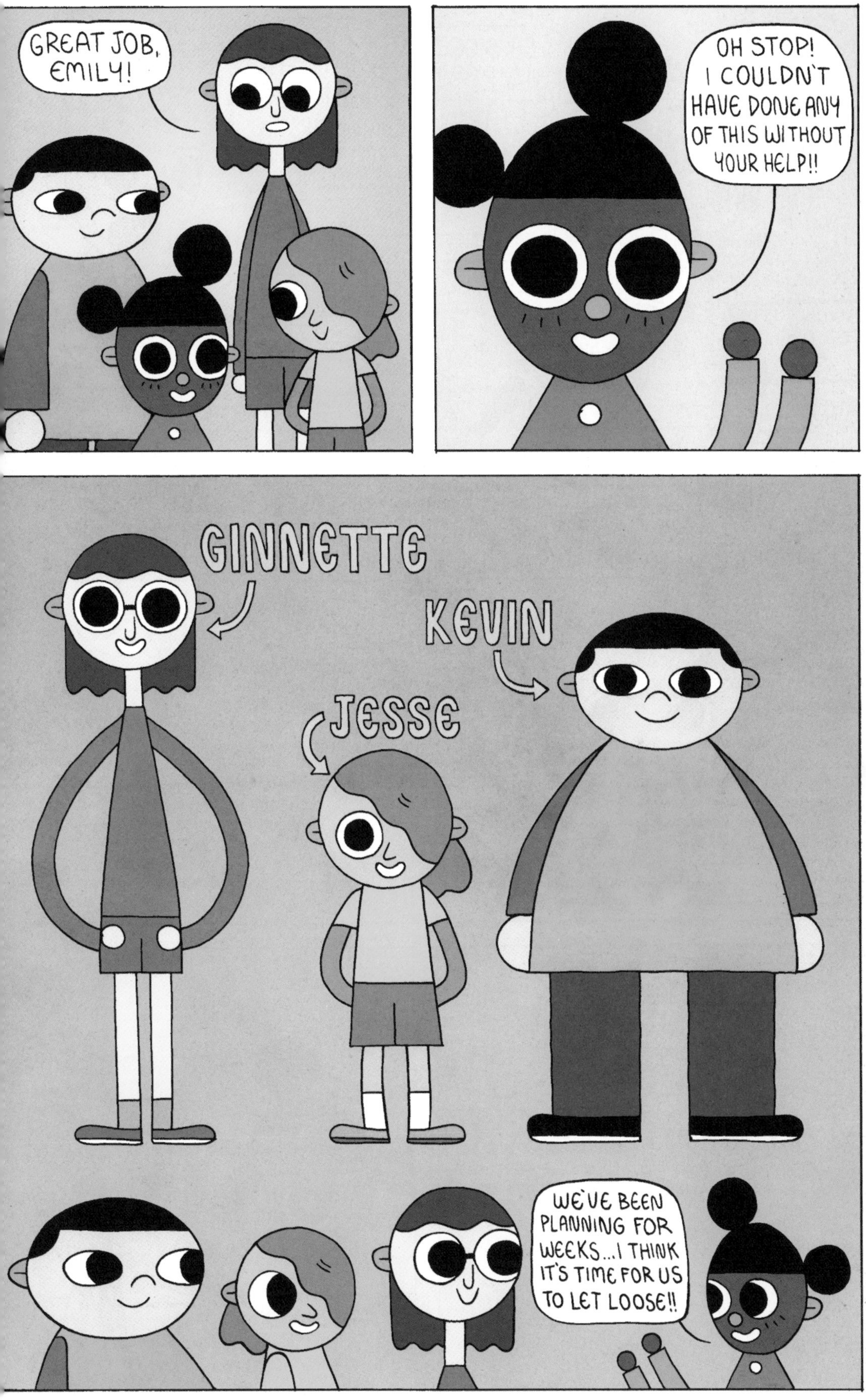
GREAT JOB, EMILY!
OH STOP! I COULDN'T HAVE DONE ANY OF THIS WITHOUT YOUR HELP!!
GINNETTE
KEVIN
JESSE
WE'VE BEEN PLANNING FOR WEEKS...I THINK IT'S TIME FOR US TO LET LOOSE!!

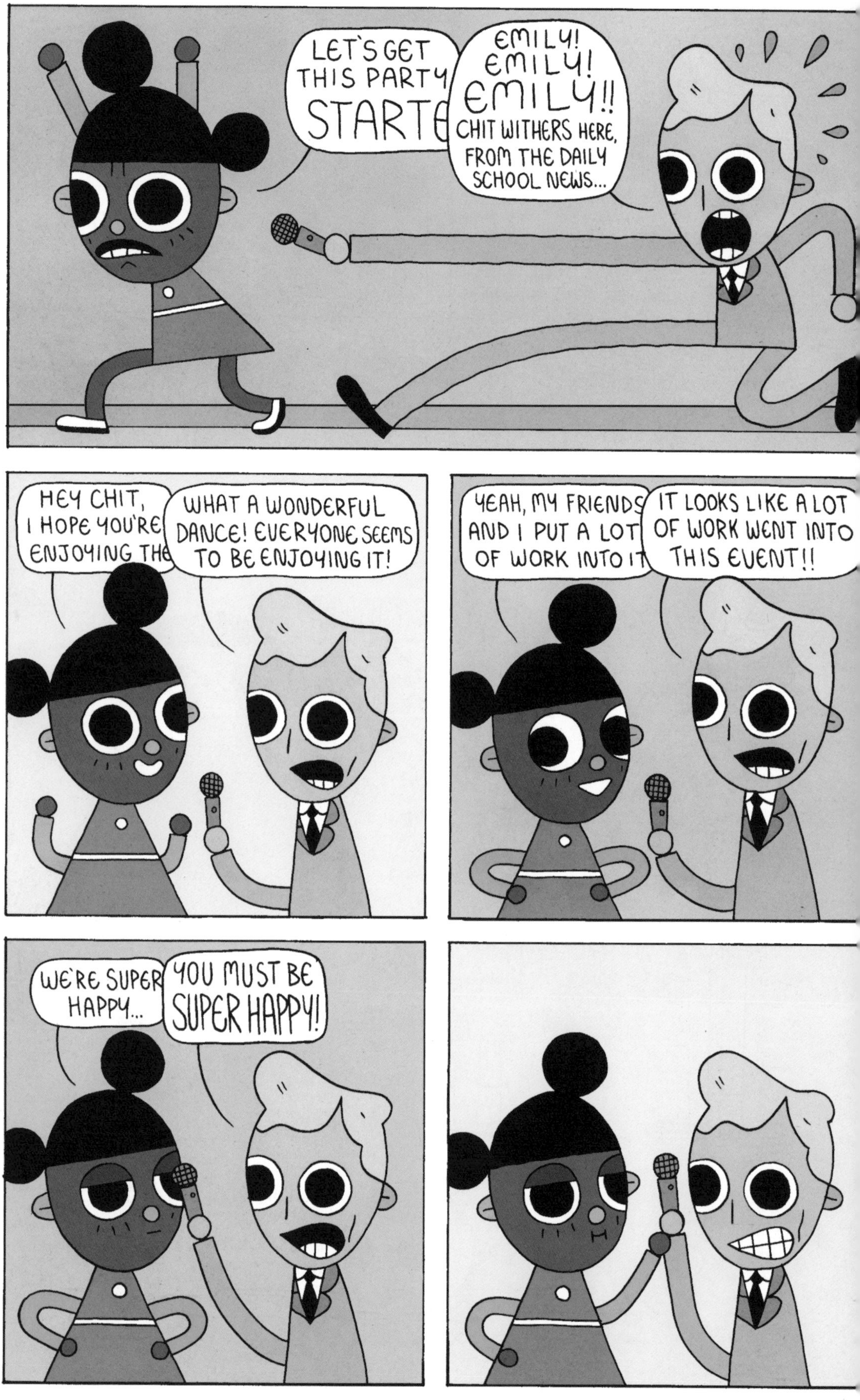
LET'S GET THIS PARTY STARTE
EMILY! EMILY! EMILY!! CHIT WITHERS HERE, FROM THE DAILY SCHOOL NEWS...
HEY CHIT, I HOPE YOU'RE ENJOYING THE
WHAT A WONDERFUL DANCE! EVERYONE SEEMS TO BE ENJOYING IT!
YEAH, MY FRIENDS AND I PUT A LOT OF WORK INTO IT
IT LOOKS LIKE A LOT OF WORK WENT INTO THIS EVENT!!
WE'RE SUPER HAPPY...
YOU MUST BE SUPER HAPPY!

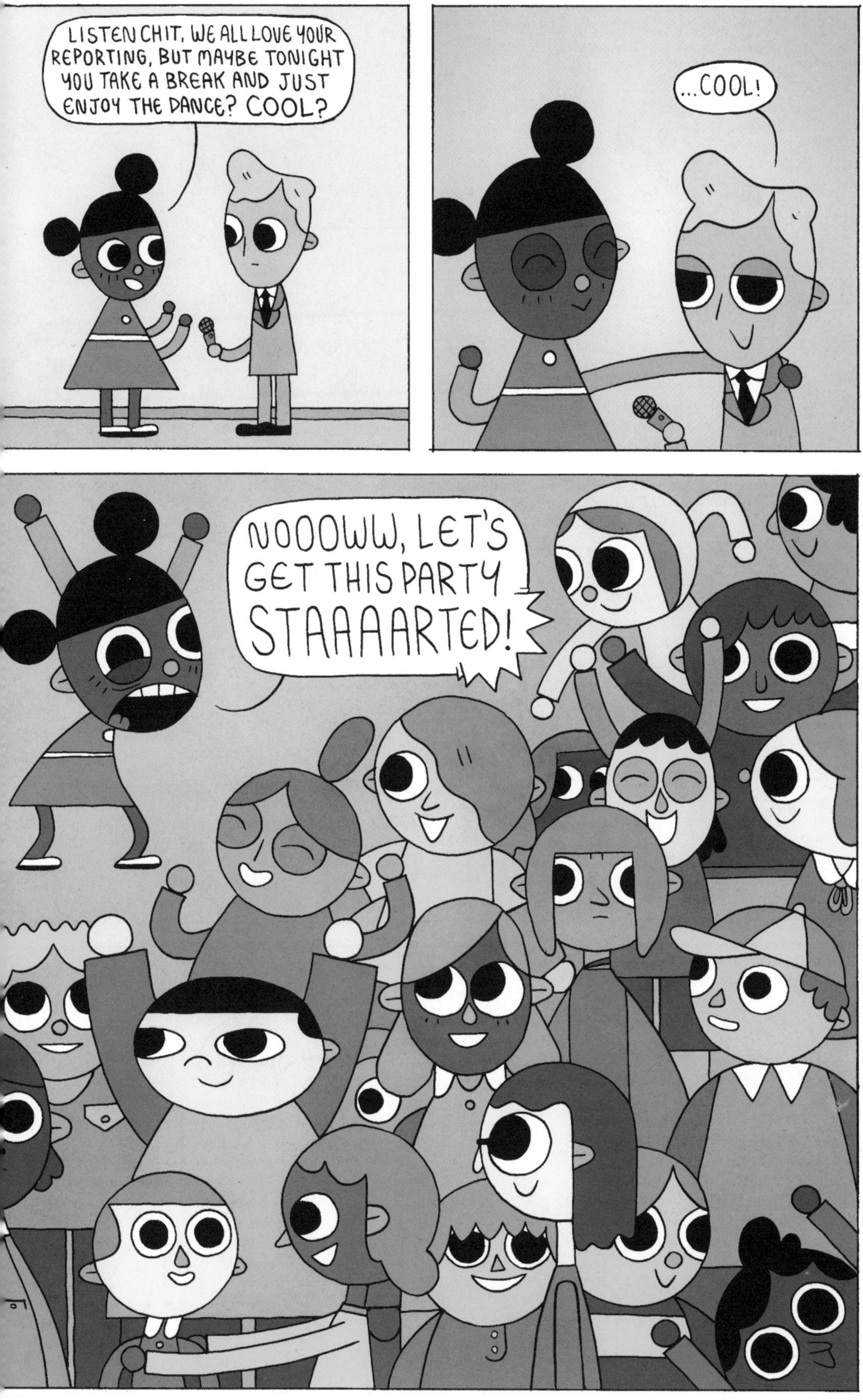
LISTEN CHIT, WE ALL LOVE YOUR REPORTING, BUT MAYBE TONIGHT YOU TAKE A BREAK AND JUST ENJOY THE DANCE? COOL?
...COOL!
NOOOWW, LET'S GET THIS PARTY STAAAARTED!

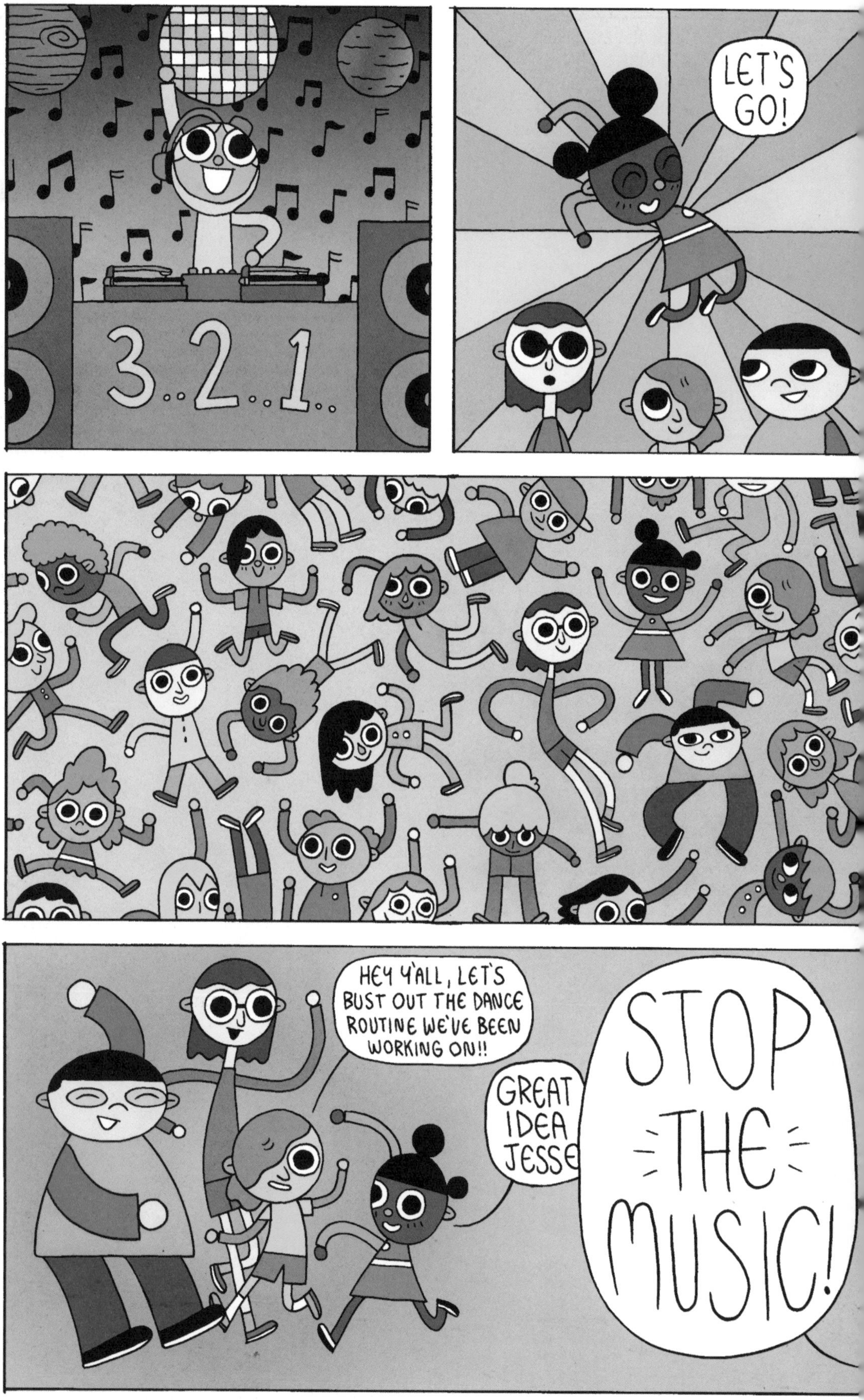

3..2..1..
LET'S GO!
HEY Y'ALL, LET'S BUST OUT THE DANCE ROUTINE WE'VE BEEN WORKING ON!!
GREAT IDEA JESSE
STOP THE MUSIC!

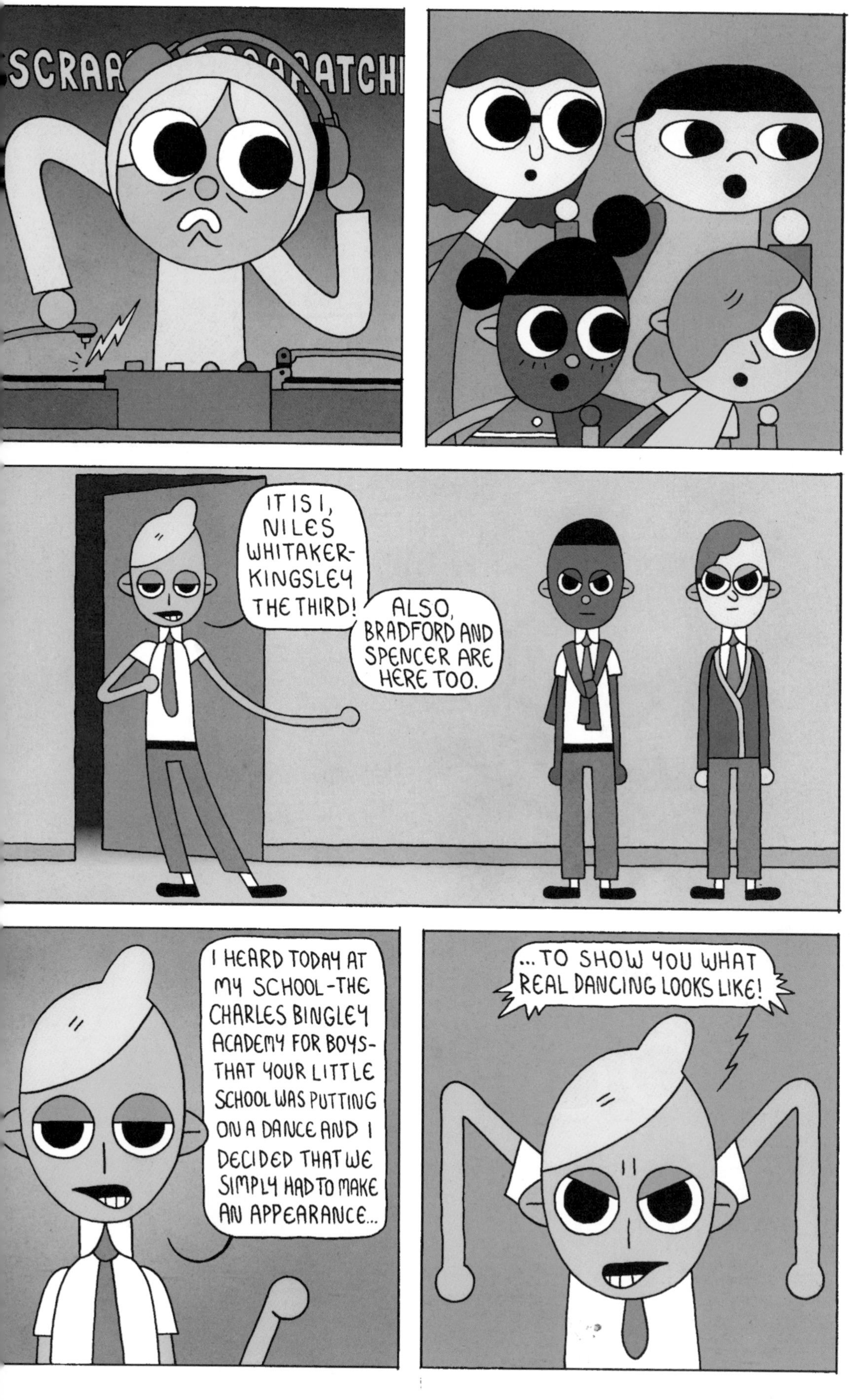
SCRAA
ATCH
IT IS I, NILES WHITAKER-KINGSLEY THE THIRD!
ALSO, BRADFORD AND SPENCER ARE HERE TOO.
I HEARD TODAY AT MY SCHOOL - THE CHARLES BINGLEY ACADEMY FOR BOYS - THAT YOUR LITTLE SCHOOL WAS PUTTING ON A DANCE AND I DECIDED THAT WE SIMPLY HAD TO MAKE AN APPEARANCE...
...TO SHOW YOU WHAT REAL DANCING LOOKS LIKE!

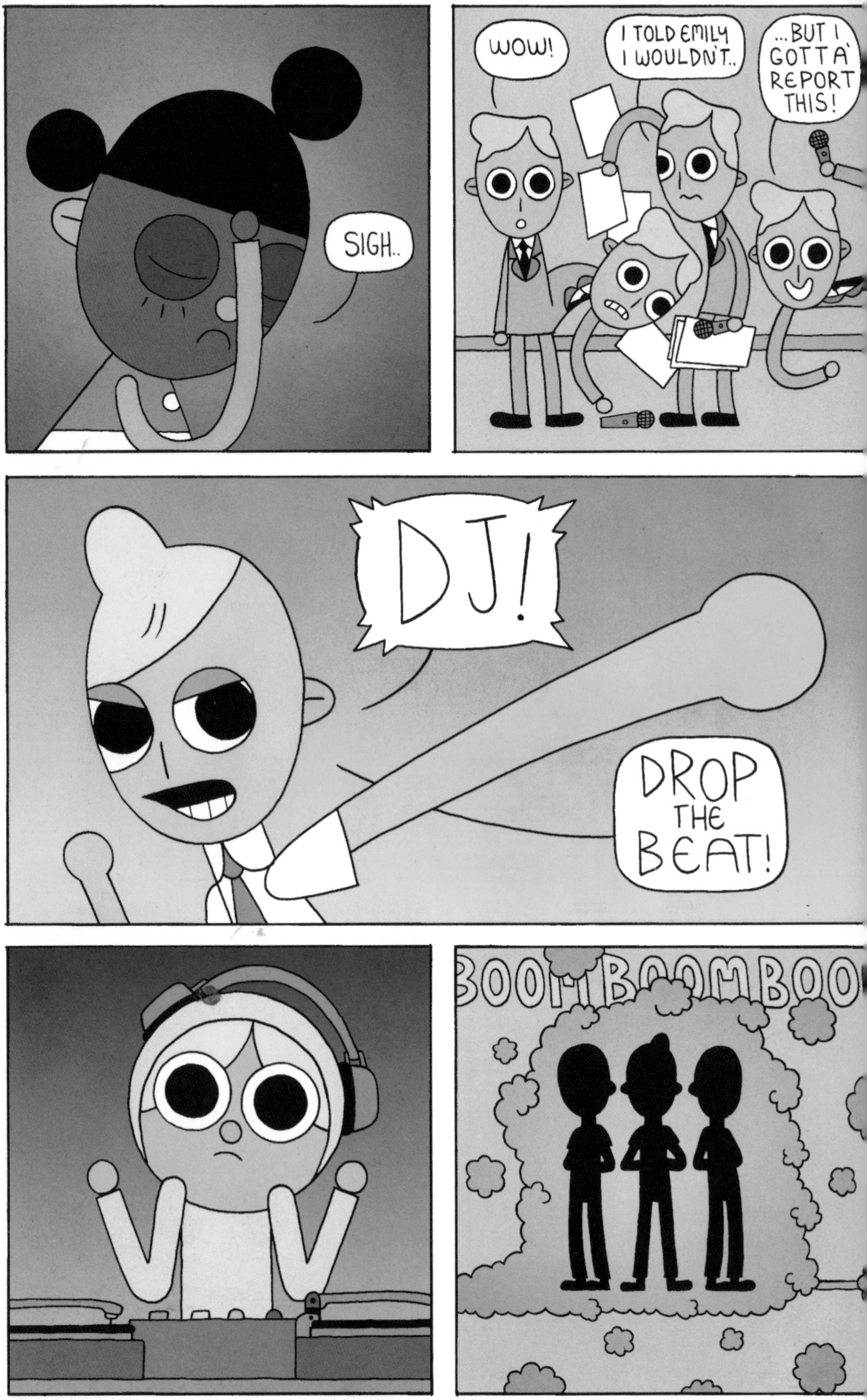
SIGH..
WOW!
I TOLD EMILY I WOULDN'T..
...BUT I GOTTA REPORT THIS!
DJ!
DROP THE BEAT!
BOOMBOOMBOO

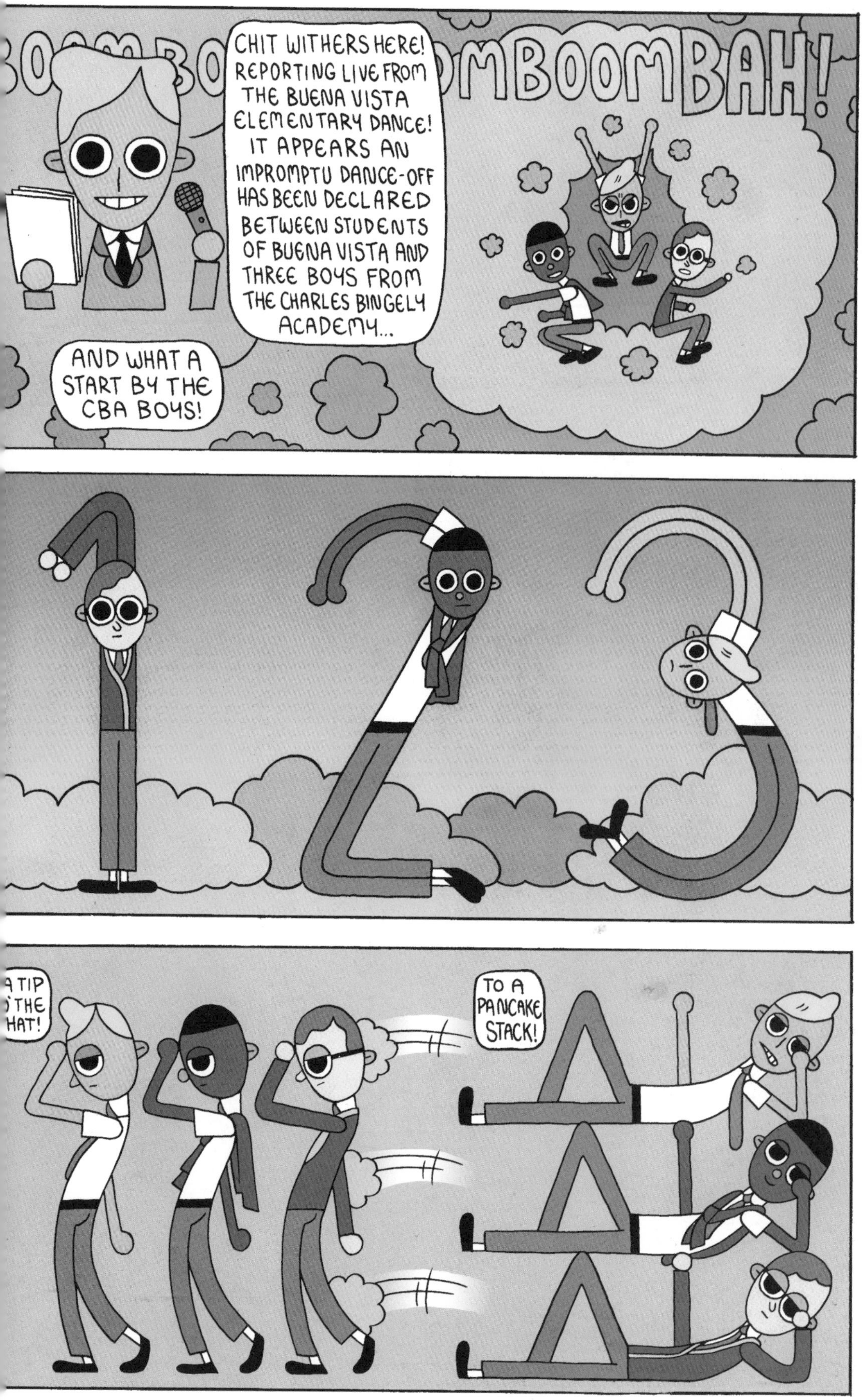
BOOMBOOMBOOMBOOMBAH!
CHIT WITHERS HERE! REPORTING LIVE FROM THE BUENA VISTA ELEMENTARY DANCE! IT APPEARS AN IMPROMPTU DANCE-OFF HAS BEEN DECLARED BETWEEN STUDENTS OF BUENA VISTA AND THREE BOYS FROM THE CHARLES BINGELY ACADEMY...
AND WHAT A START BY THE CBA BOYS!
A TIP 'THE HAT!
TO A PANCAKE STACK!

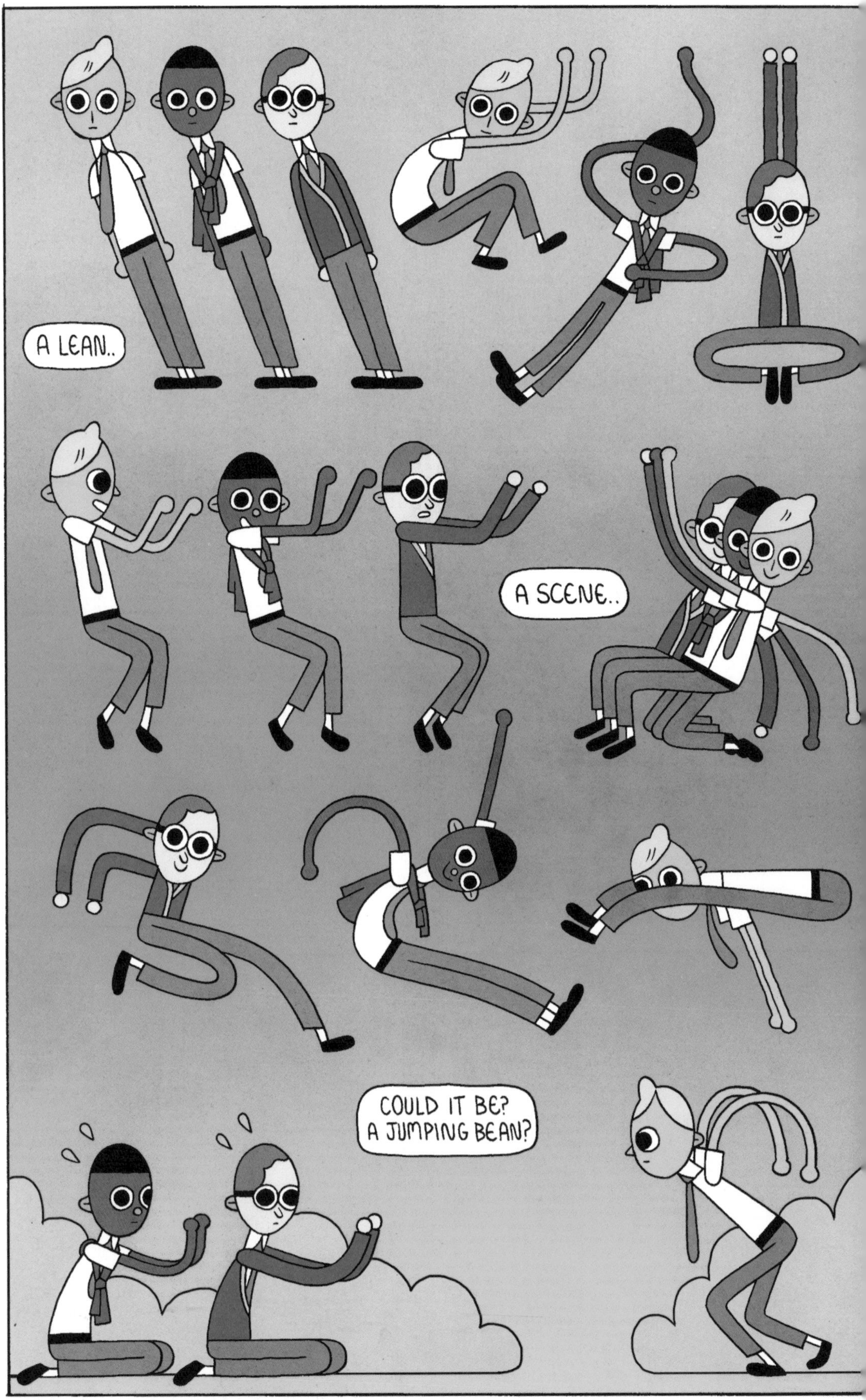
A LEAN..
A SCENE..
COULD IT BE?
A JUMPING BEAN?

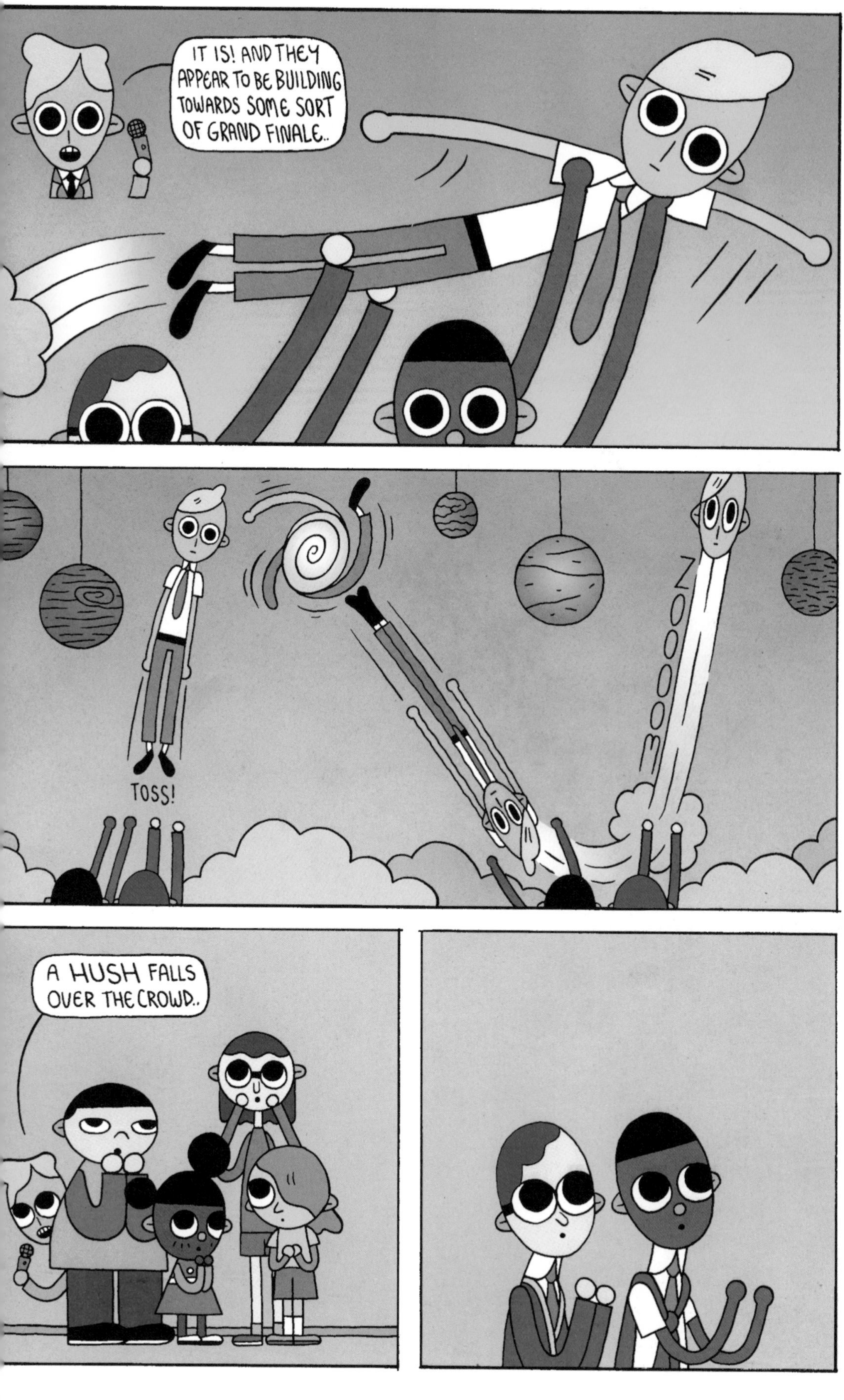
IT IS! AND THEY APPEAR TO BE BUILDING TOWARDS SOME SORT OF GRAND FINALE..
TOSS!
ZOOOOOOOM
A HUSH FALLS OVER THE CROWD..

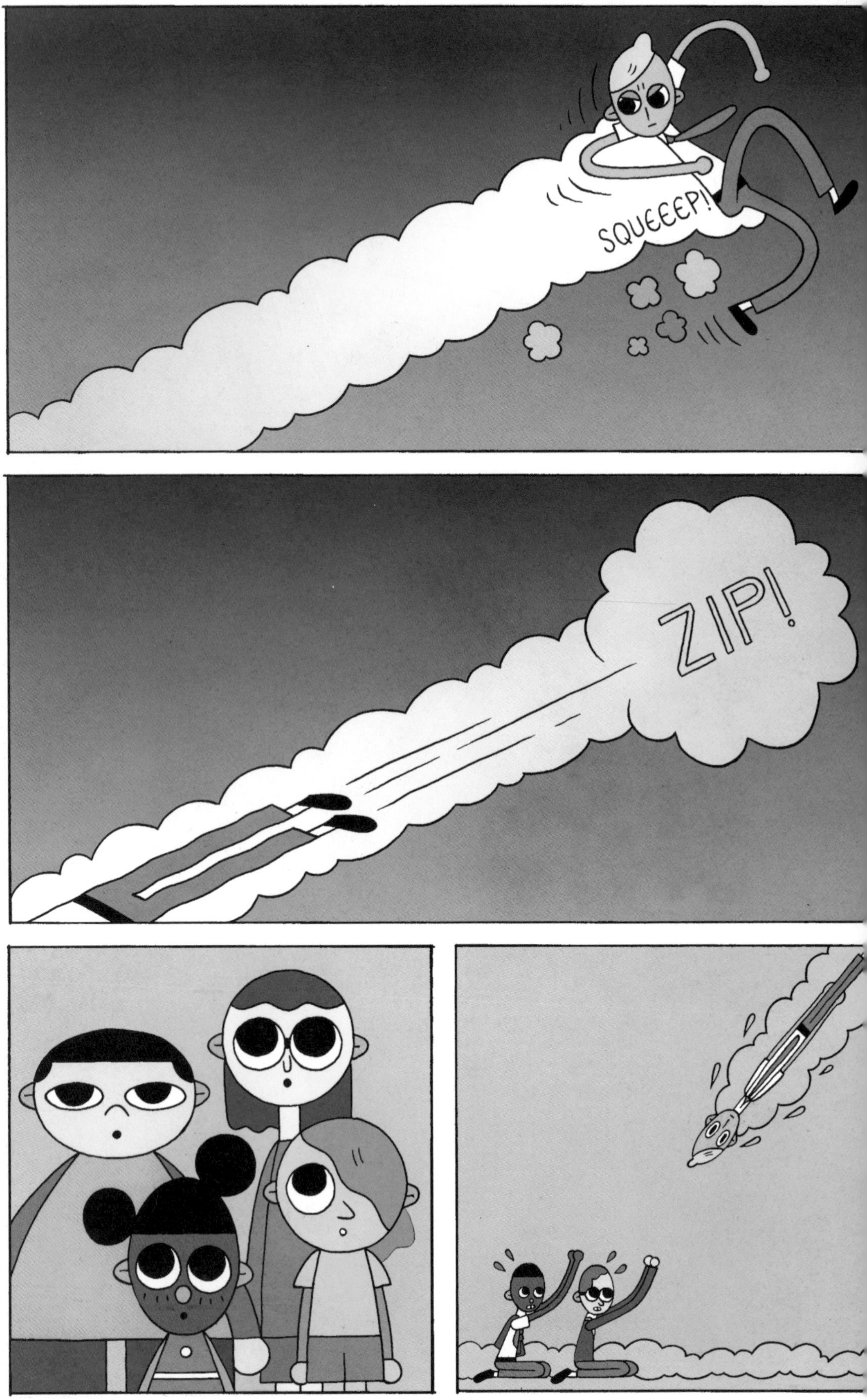
SQUEEEP!
ZIP!

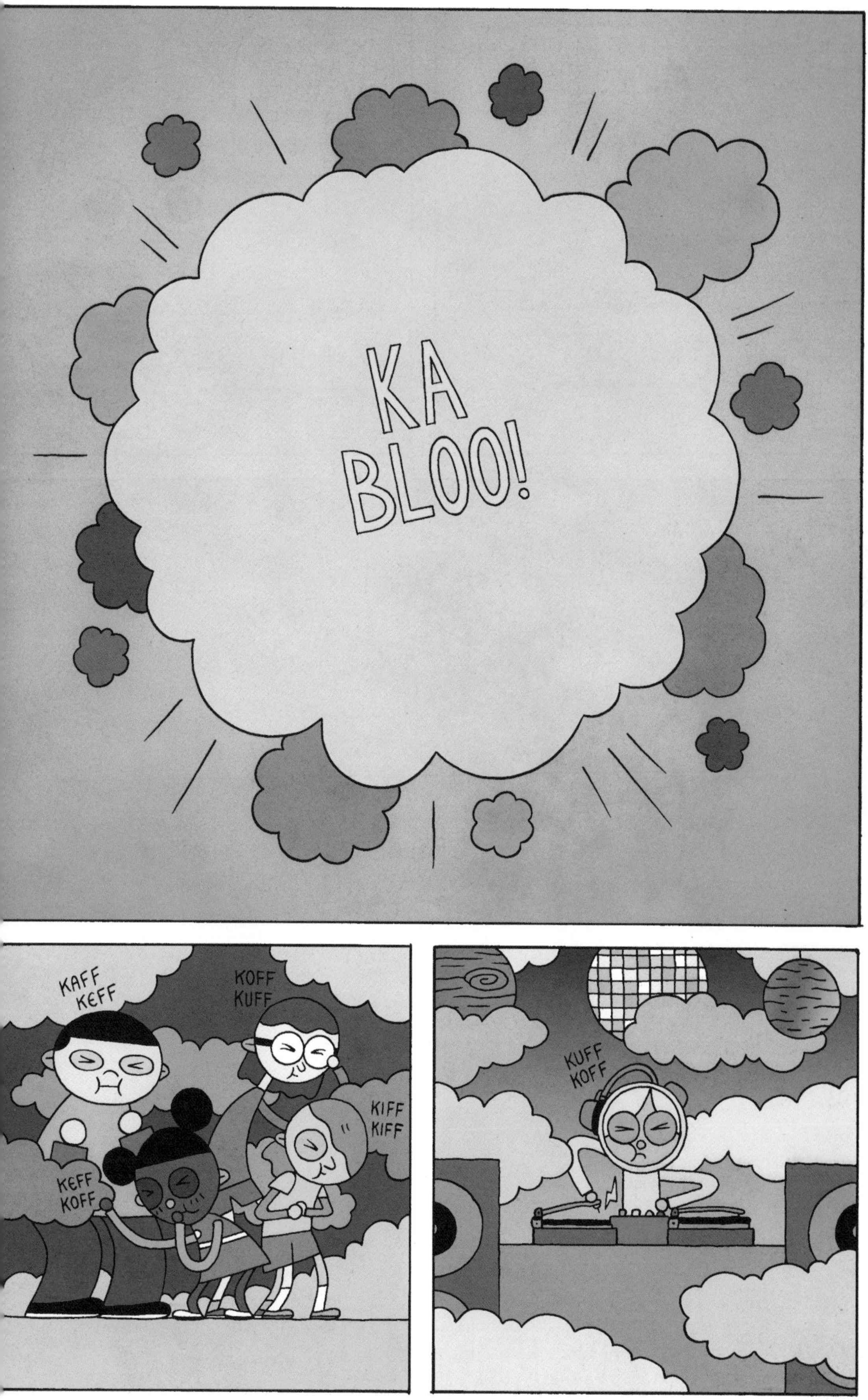
KA BLOO!
KAFF KEFF
KOFF KUFF
KIFF KIFF
KEFF KOFF
KUFF KOFF

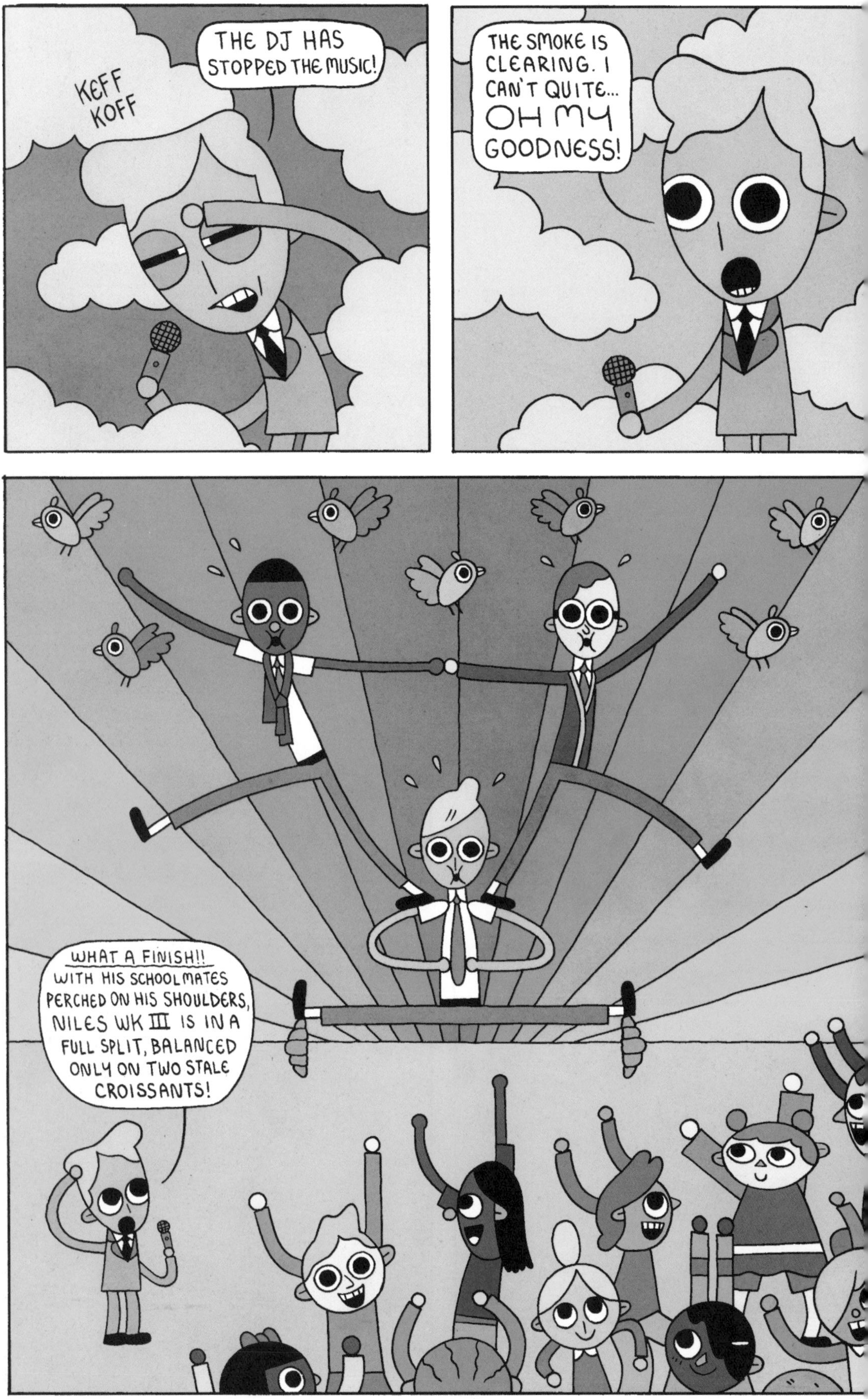
KEFF KOFF
THE DJ HAS STOPPED THE MUSIC!
THE SMOKE IS CLEARING. I CAN'T QUITE... OH MY GOODNESS!
WHAT A FINISH!! WITH HIS SCHOOLMATES PERCHED ON HIS SHOULDERS, NILES WK III IS IN A FULL SPLIT, BALANCED ONLY ON TWO STALE CROISSANTS!

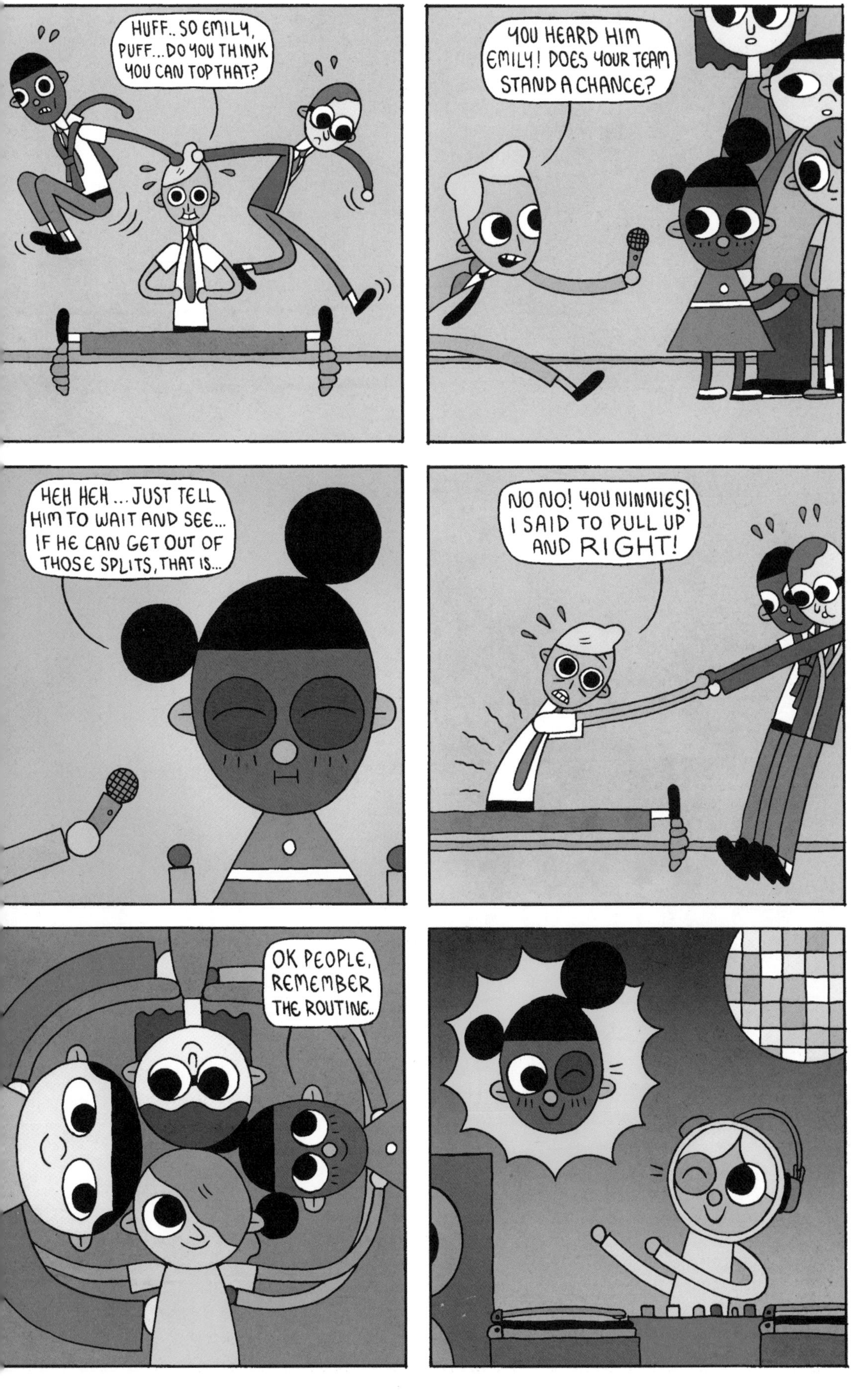
HUFF.. SO EMILY, PUFF...DO YOU THINK YOU CAN TOP THAT?
YOU HEARD HIM EMILY! DOES YOUR TEAM STAND A CHANCE?
HEH HEH ... JUST TELL HIM TO WAIT AND SEE... IF HE CAN GET OUT OF THOSE SPLITS, THAT IS...
NO NO! YOU NINNIES! I SAID TO PULL UP AND RIGHT!
OK PEOPLE, REMEMBER THE ROUTINE..

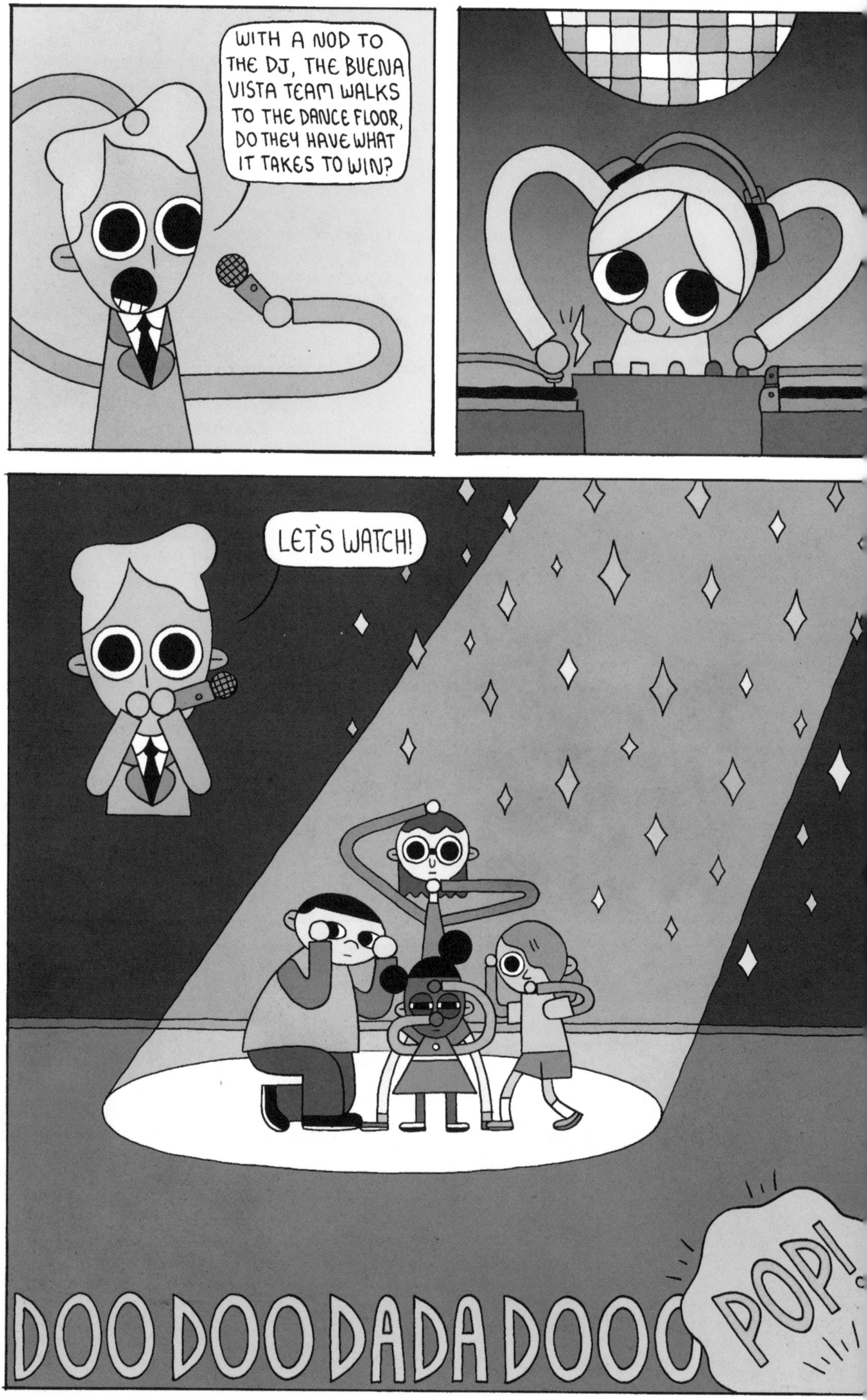
WITH A NOD TO THE DJ, THE BUENA VISTA TEAM WALKS TO THE DANCE FLOOR, DO THEY HAVE WHAT IT TAKES TO WIN?
LET'S WATCH!
DOO DOO DADA DOOO
POP!

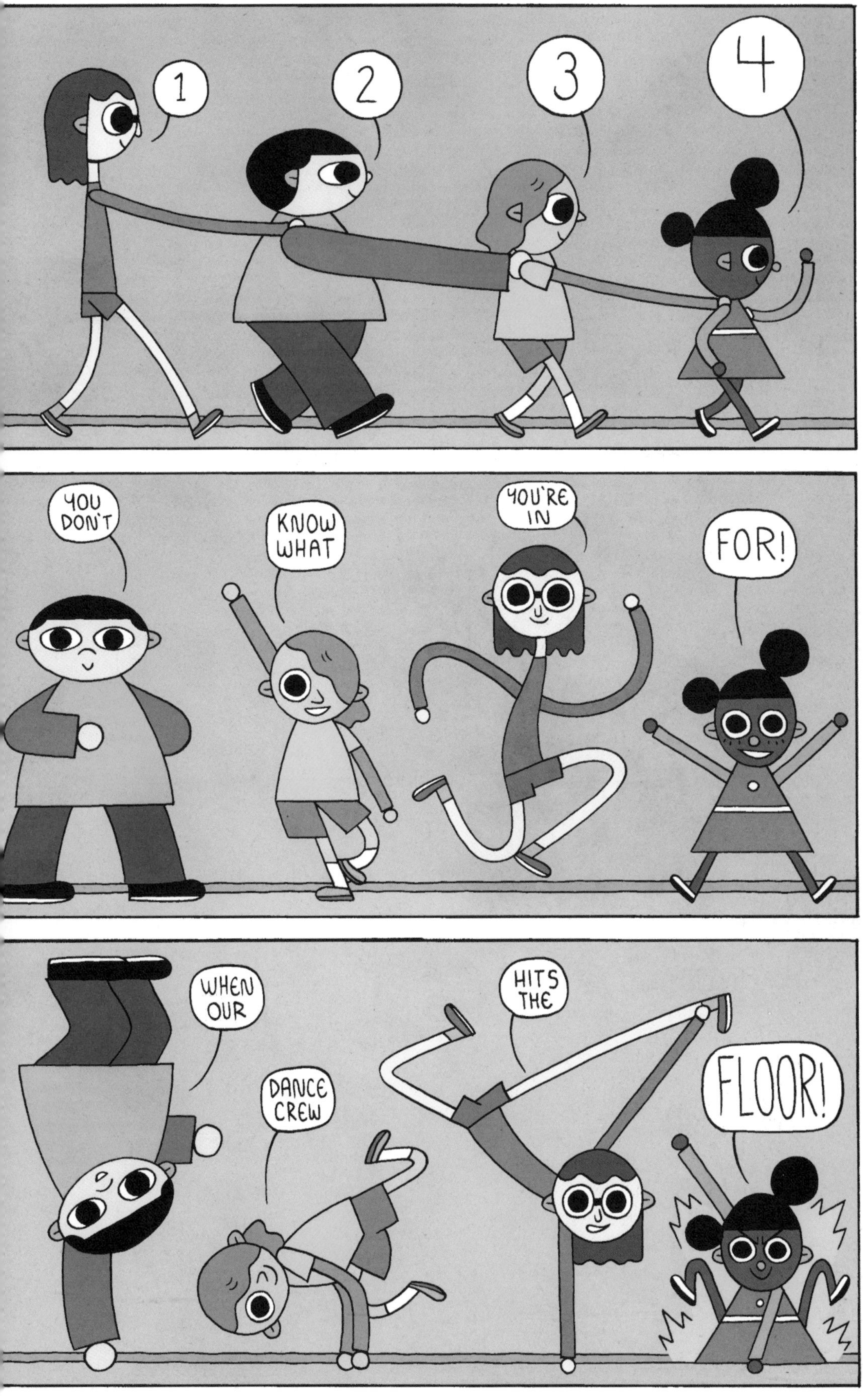
1
2
3
4
YOU DON'T
KNOW WHAT
YOU'RE IN
FOR!
WHEN OUR
DANCE CREW
HITS THE
FLOOR!

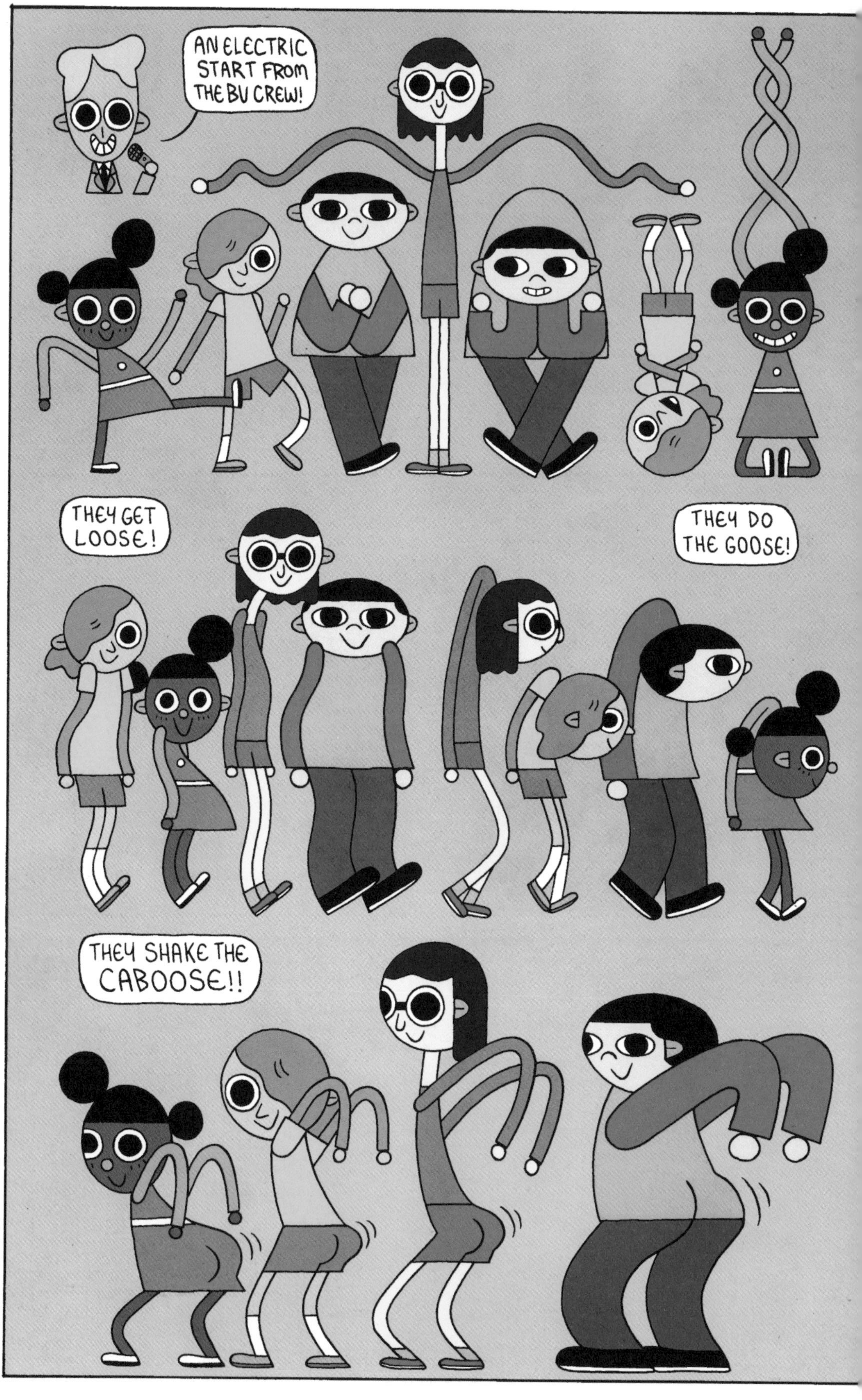
AN ELECTRIC START FROM THE BU CREW!
THEY GET LOOSE!
THEY DO THE GOOSE!
THEY SHAKE THE CABOOSE!!

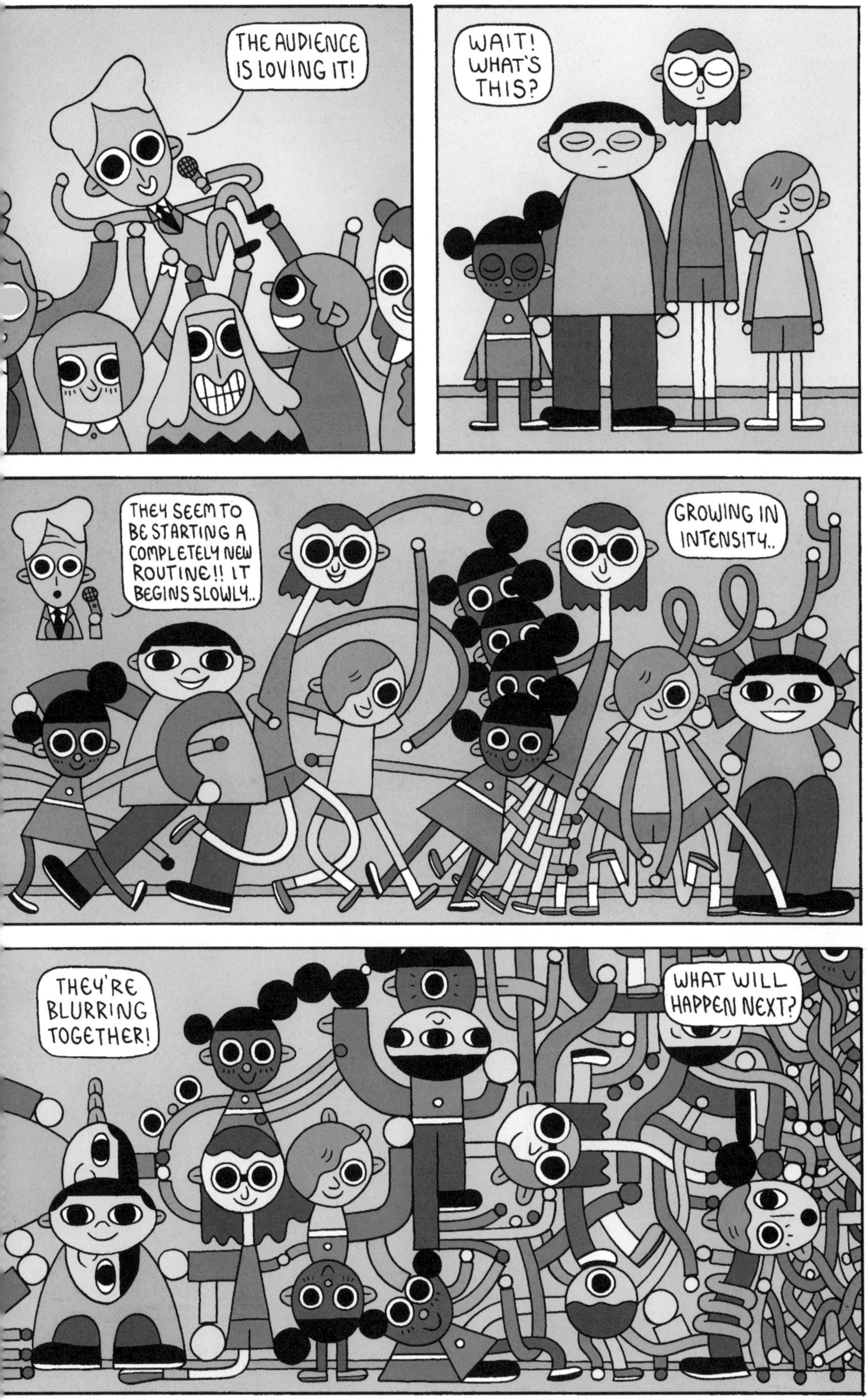
THE AUDIENCE IS LOVING IT!
WAIT! WHAT'S THIS?
THEY SEEM TO BE STARTING A COMPLETELY NEW ROUTINE!! IT BEGINS SLOWLY..
GROWING IN INTENSITY..
THEY'RE BLURRING TOGETHER!
WHAT WILL HAPPEN NEXT?

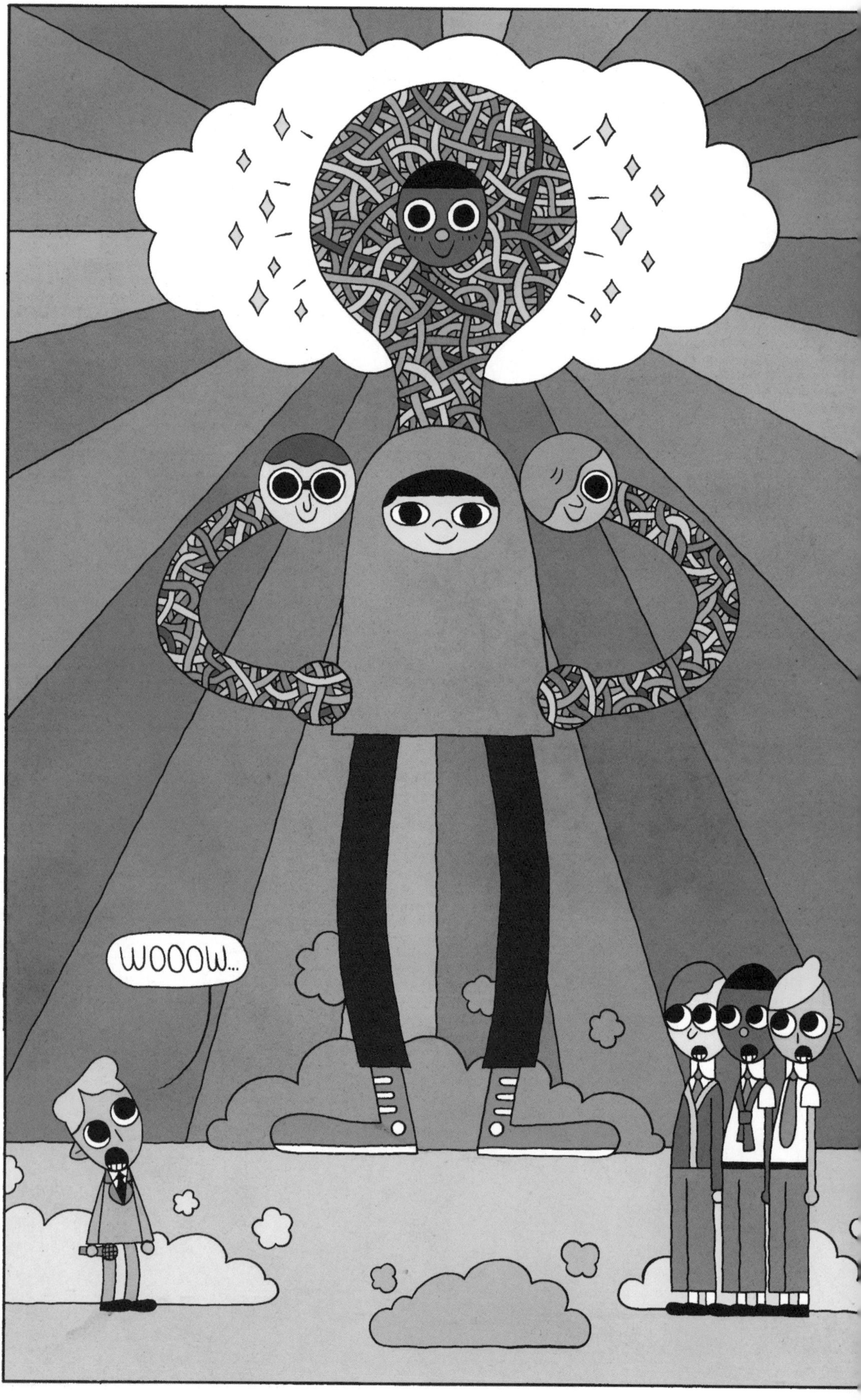
WOOOW...

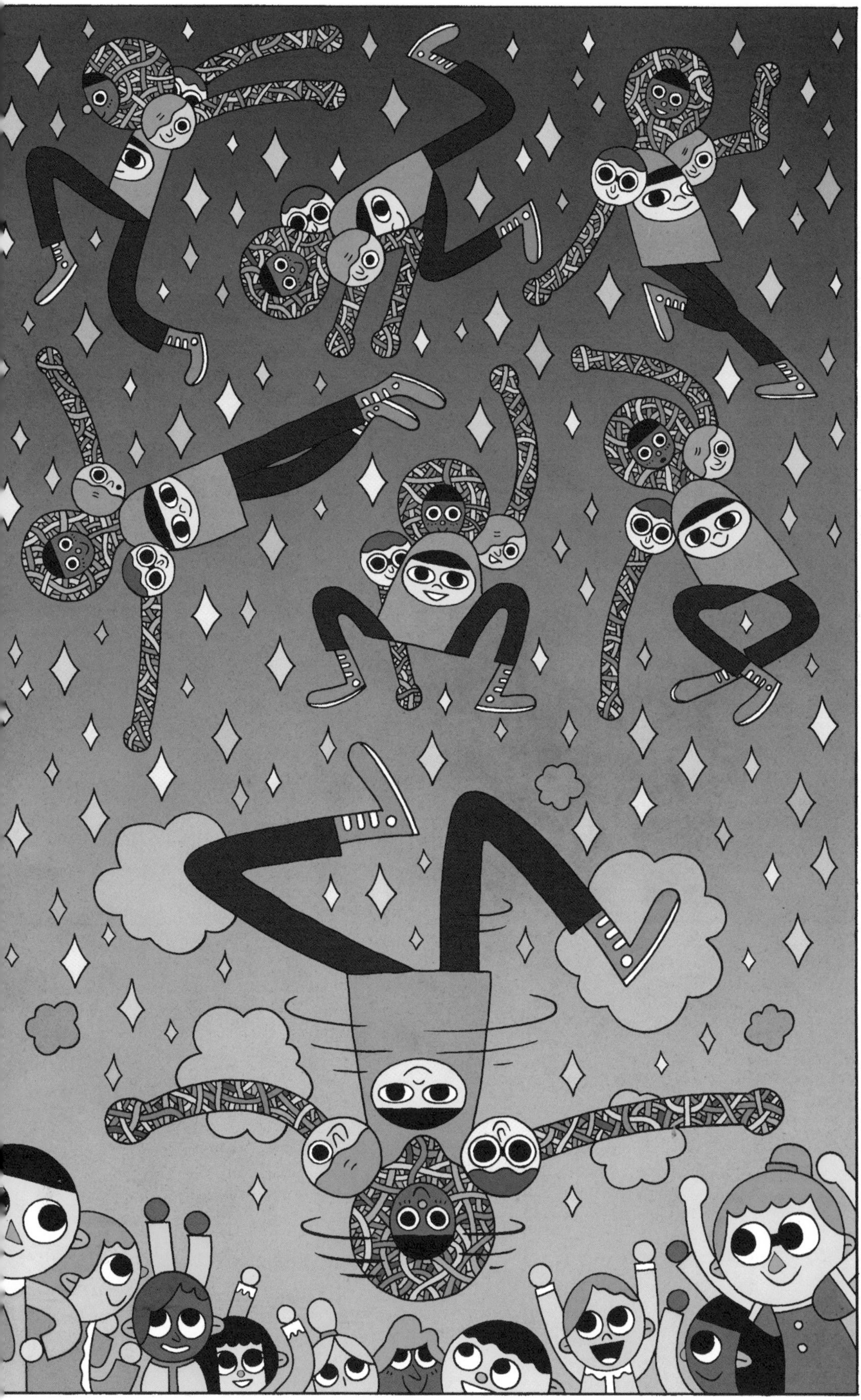

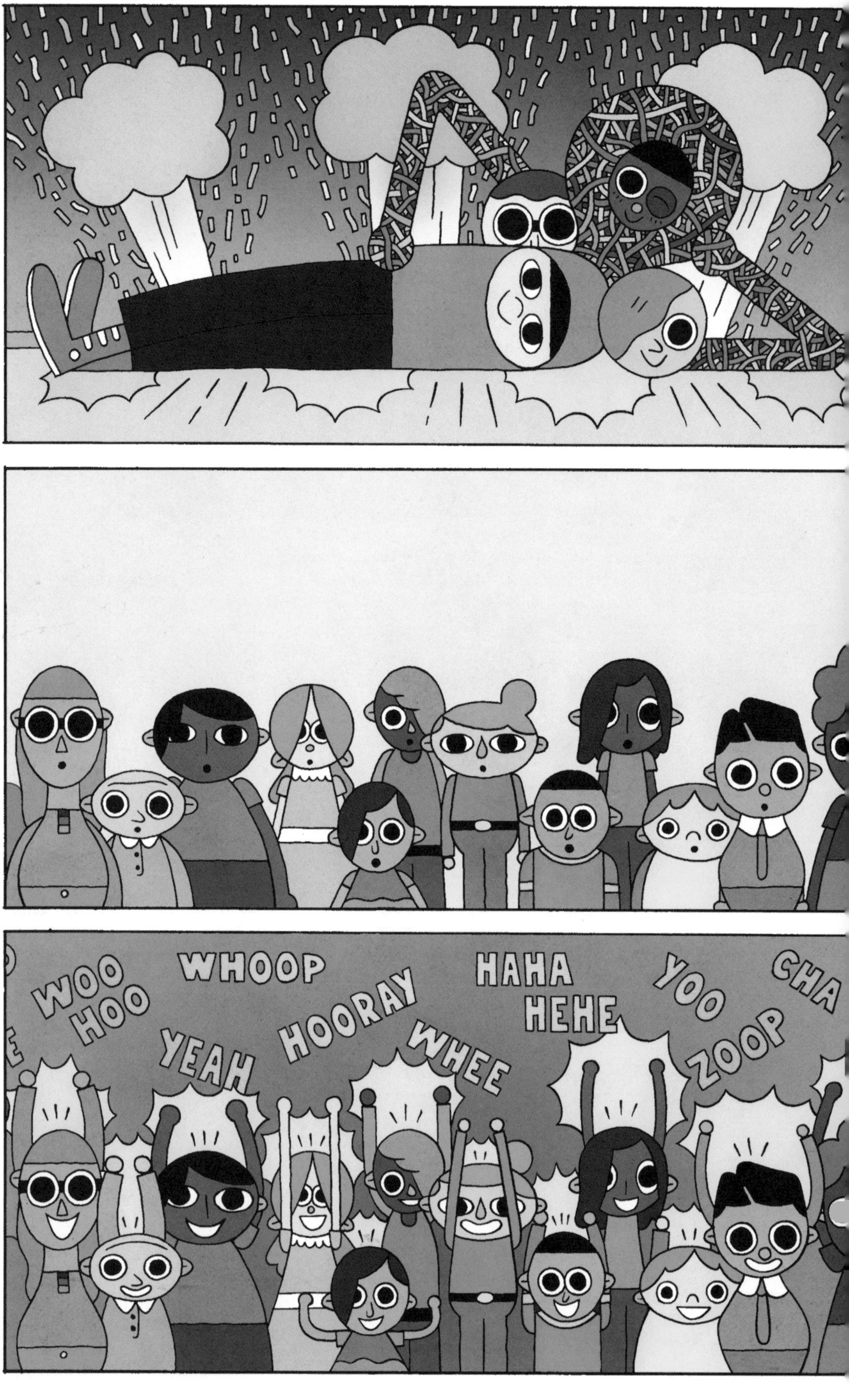
WOO
HOO
WHOOP
YEAH
HOORAY
WHEE
HAHA
HEHE
YOO
ZOOP
CHA

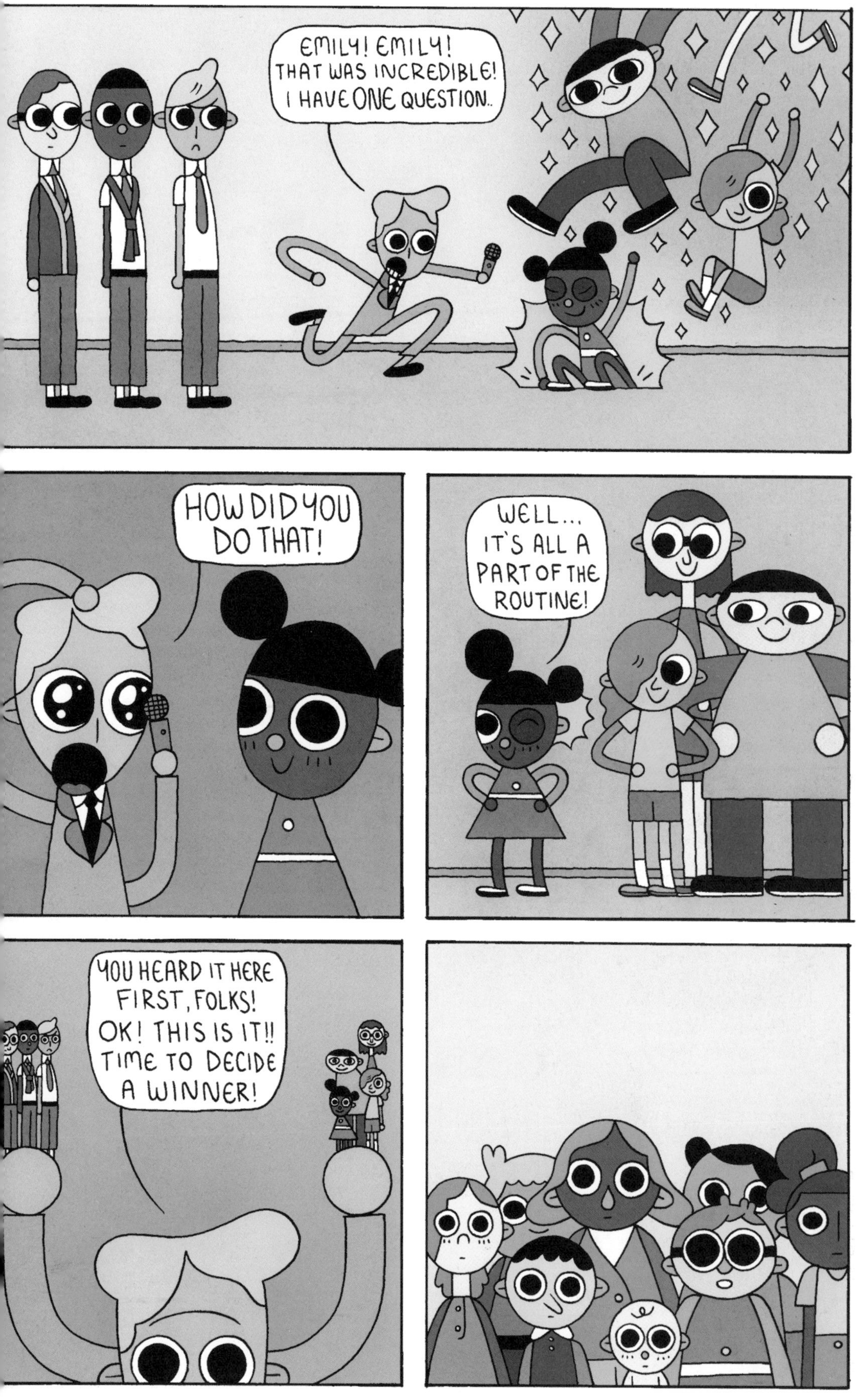
EMILY! EMILY! THAT WAS INCREDIBLE! I HAVE ONE QUESTION..
HOW DID YOU DO THAT!
WELL... IT'S ALL A PART OF THE ROUTINE!
YOU HEARD IT HERE FIRST, FOLKS! OK! THIS IS IT!! TIME TO DECIDE A WINNER!

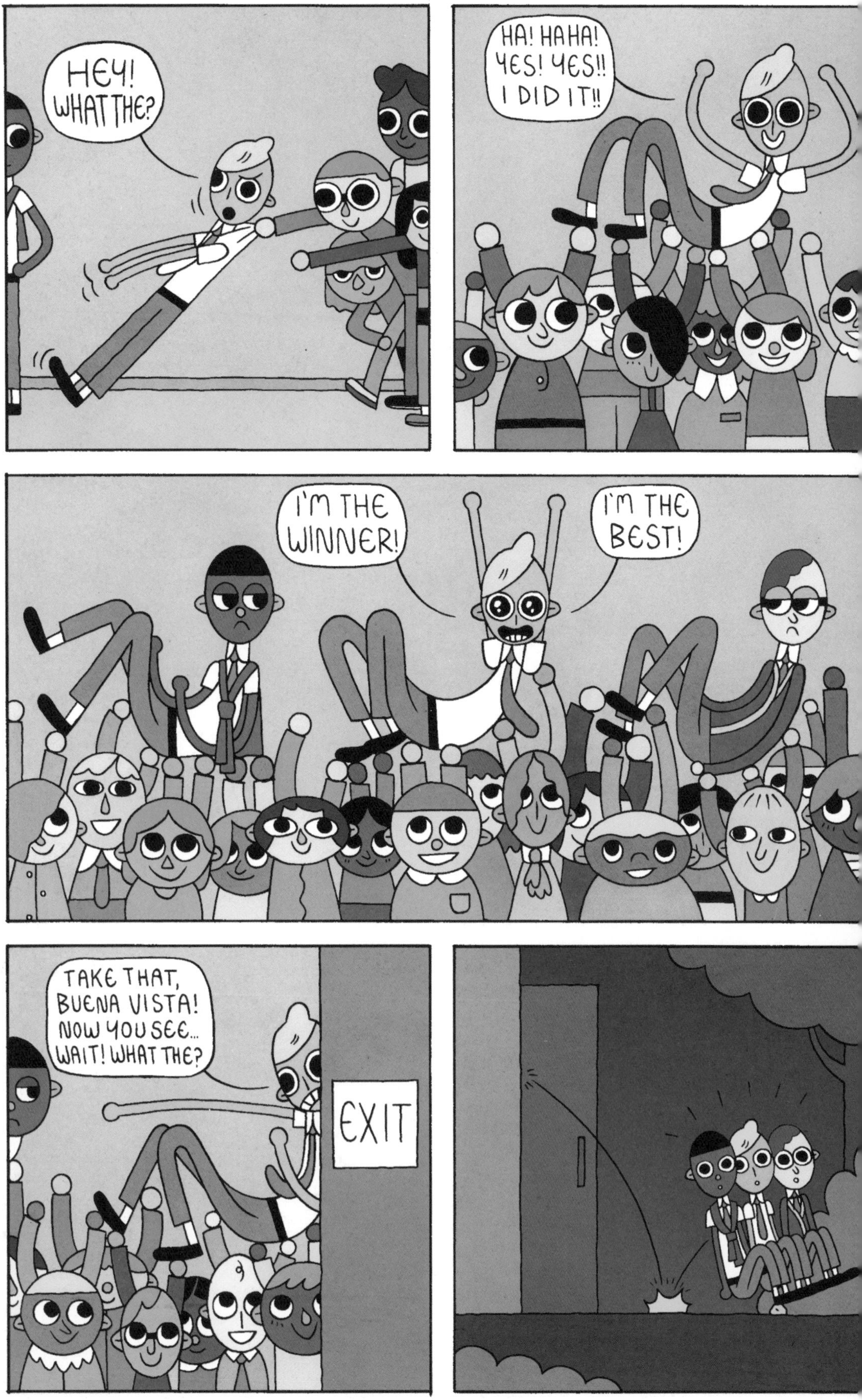
HEY! WHAT THE?
HA! HAHA! YES! YES!! I DID IT!!
I'M THE WINNER!
I'M THE BEST!
TAKE THAT, BUENA VISTA! NOW YOU SEE... WAIT! WHAT THE?
EXIT

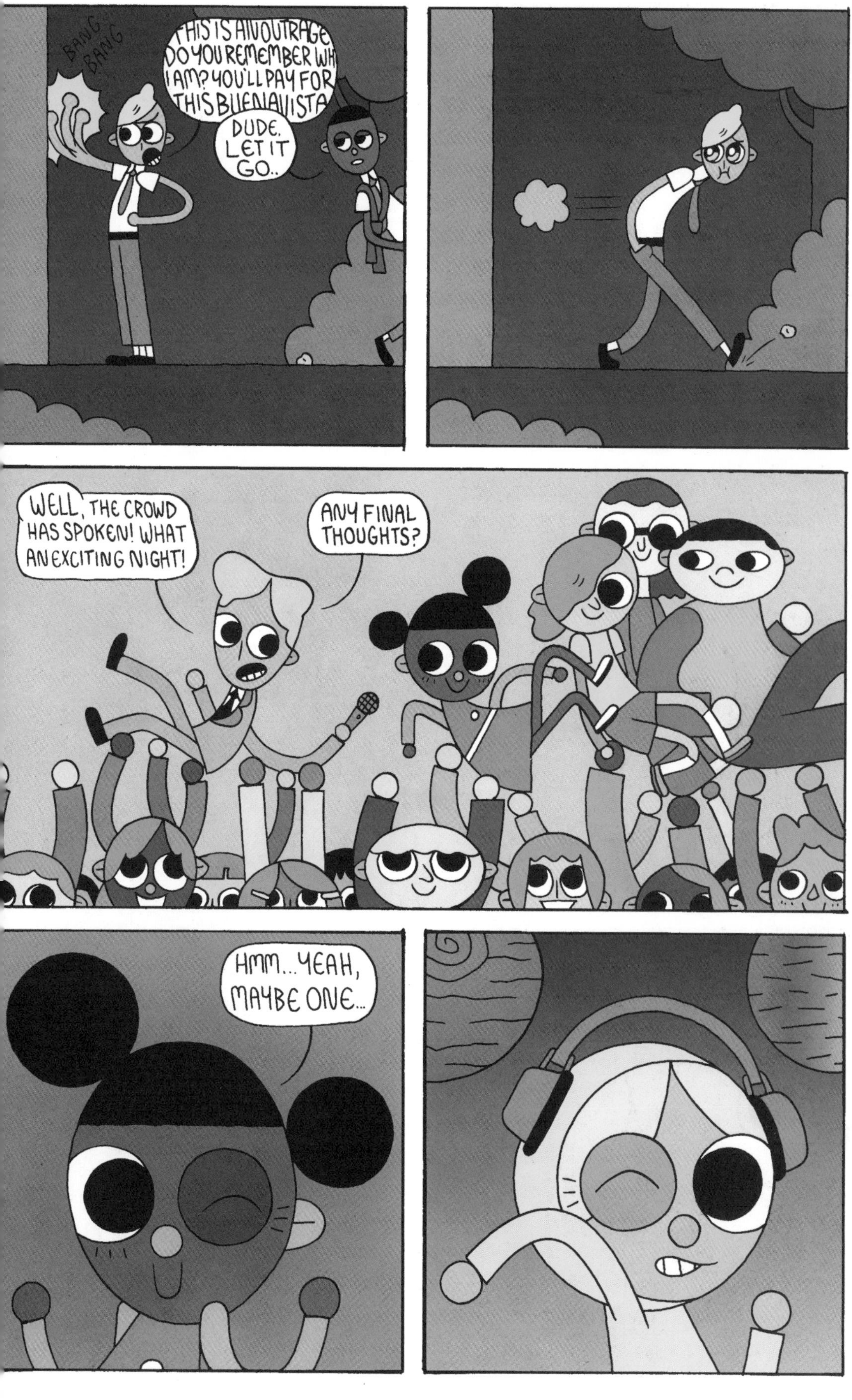
BANG BANG
THIS IS AN OUTRAGE! DO YOU REMEMBER WH I AM? YOU'LL PAY FOR THIS BUENAVISTA
DUDE. LET IT GO..
WELL, THE CROWD HAS SPOKEN! WHAT AN EXCITING NIGHT!
ANY FINAL THOUGHTS?
HMM... YEAH, MAYBE ONE...

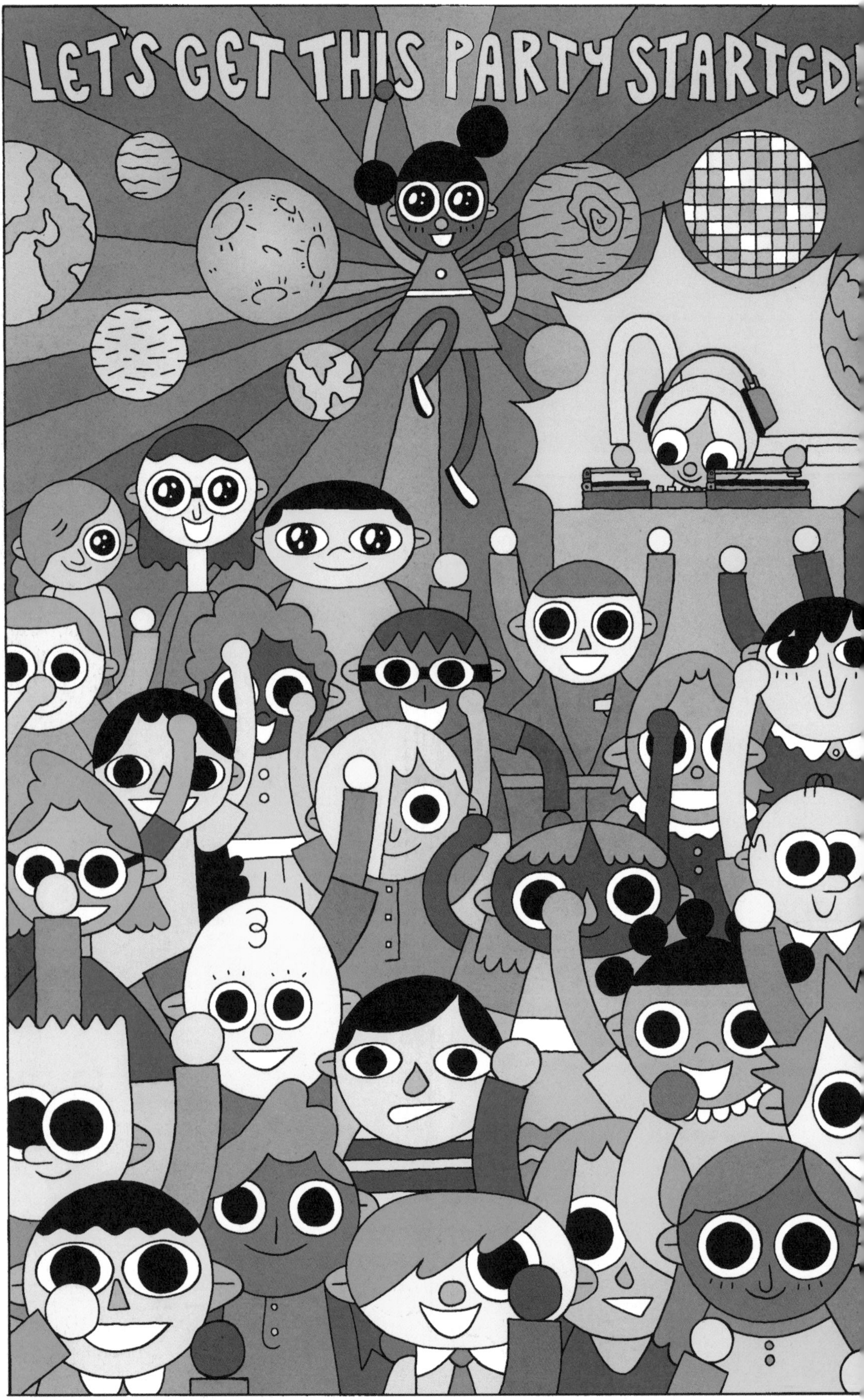
LET'S GET THIS PARTY STARTED!

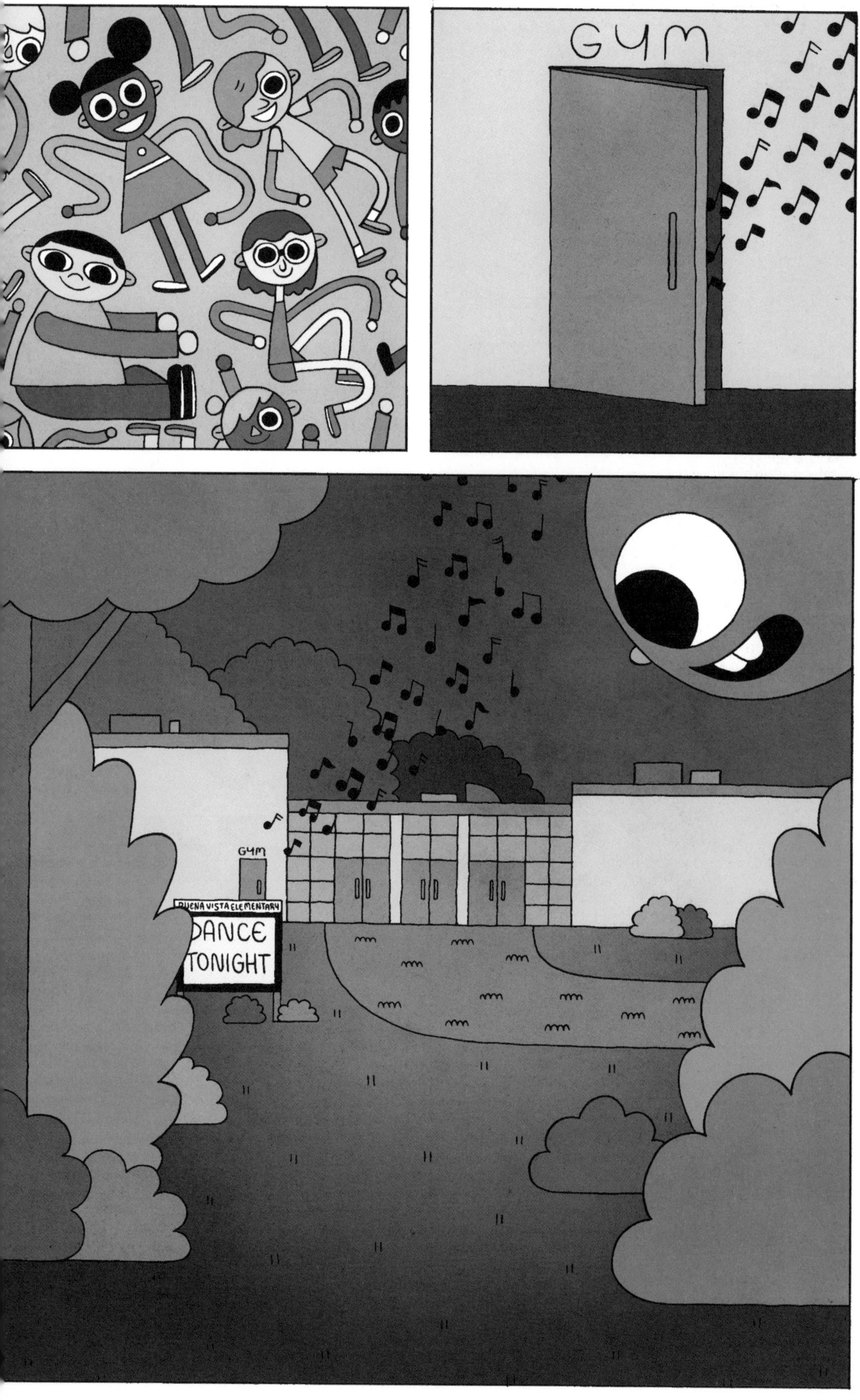
GYM
GYM
BUENA VISTA ELEMENTARY
DANCE
TONIGHT

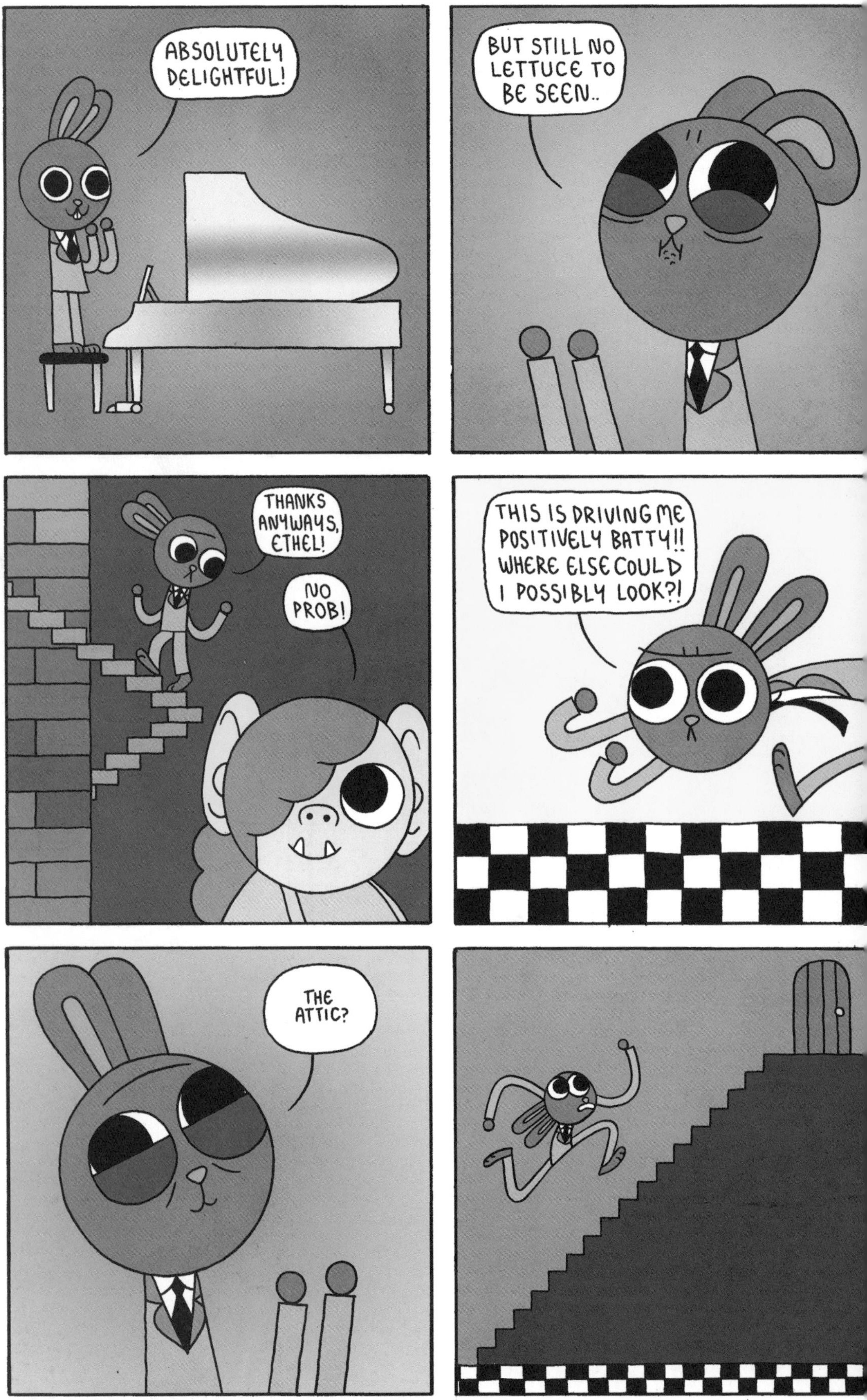
ABSOLUTELY DELIGHTFUL!
BUT STILL NO LETTUCE TO BE SEEN..
THANKS ANYWAYS, ETHEL!
NO PROB!
THIS IS DRIVING ME POSITIVELY BATTY!! WHERE ELSE COULD I POSSIBLY LOOK?!
THE ATTIC?

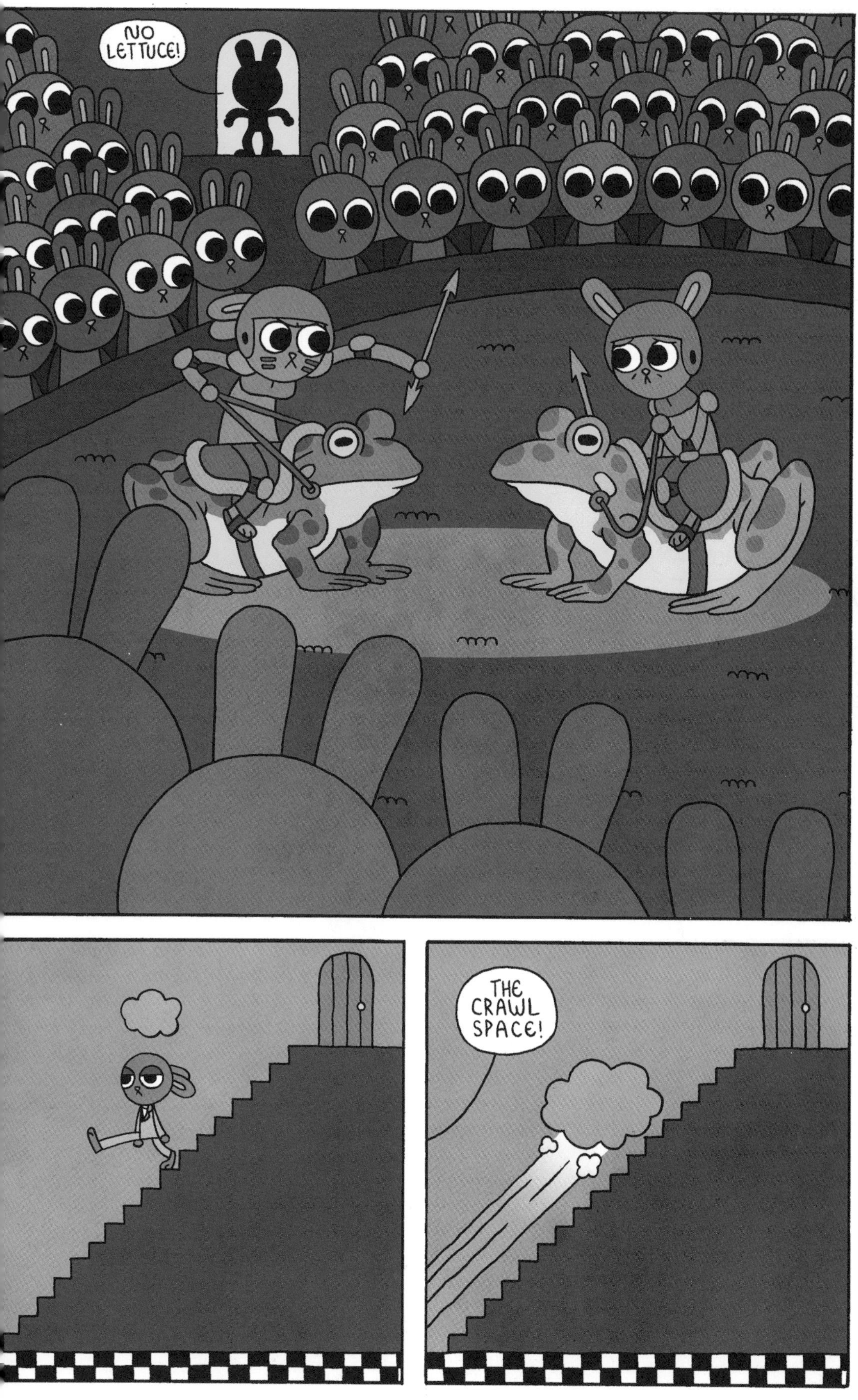
NO LETTUCE!
THE CRAWL SPACE!

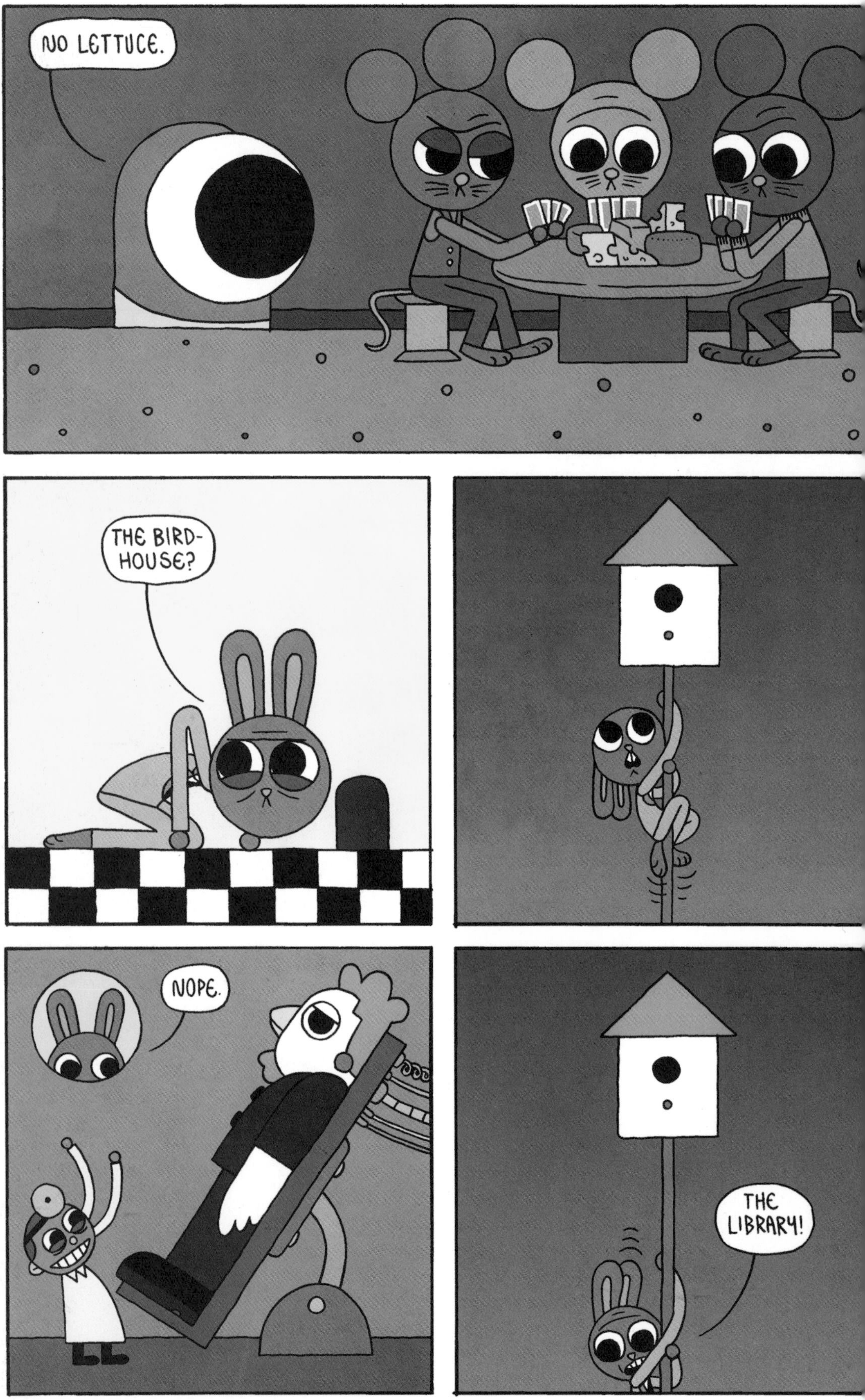
NO LETTUCE.
THE BIRD-HOUSE?
NOPE.
THE LIBRARY!

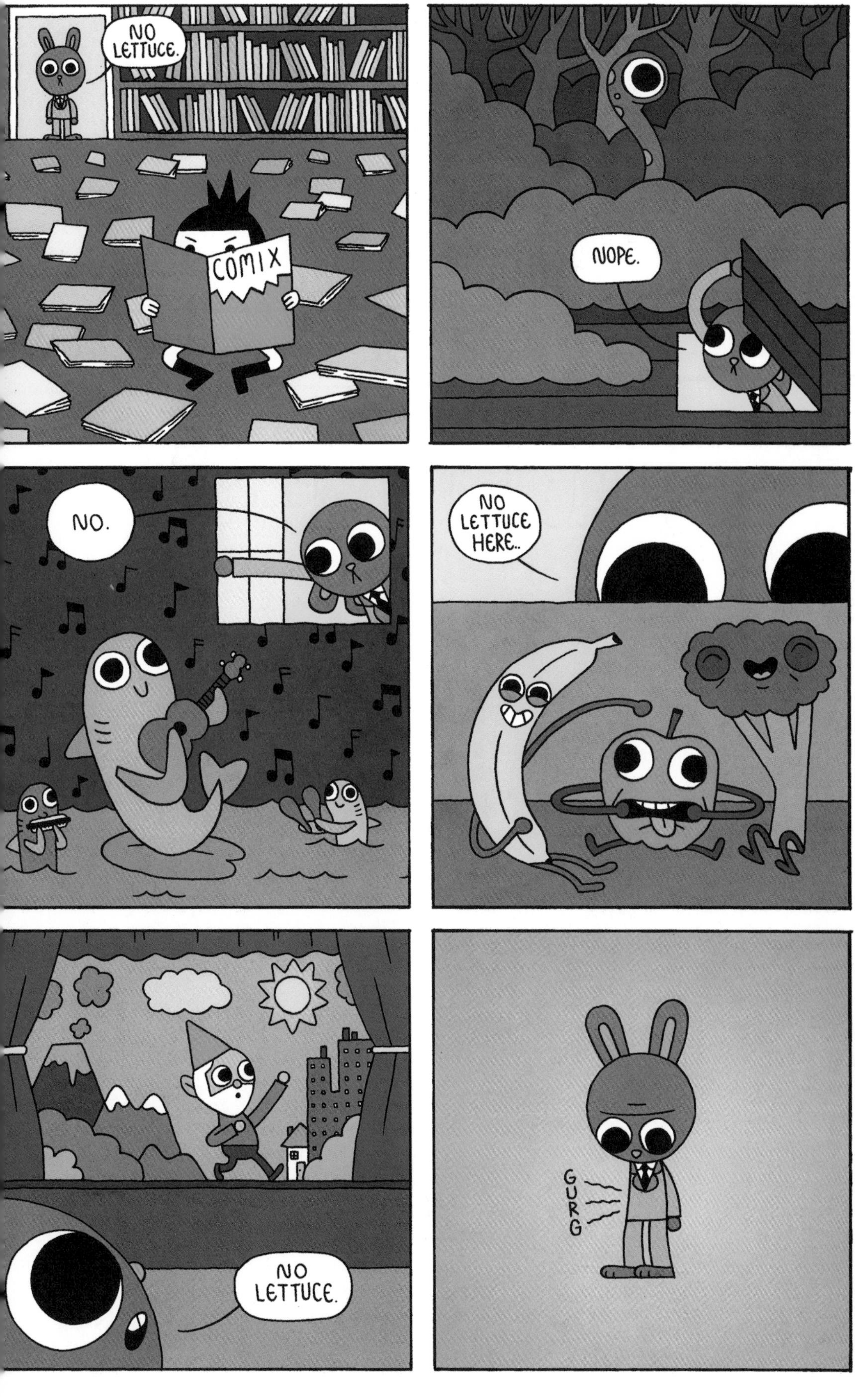
NO LETTUCE.
COMIX
NOPE.
NO.
NO LETTUCE HERE..
NO LETTUCE.
GURG

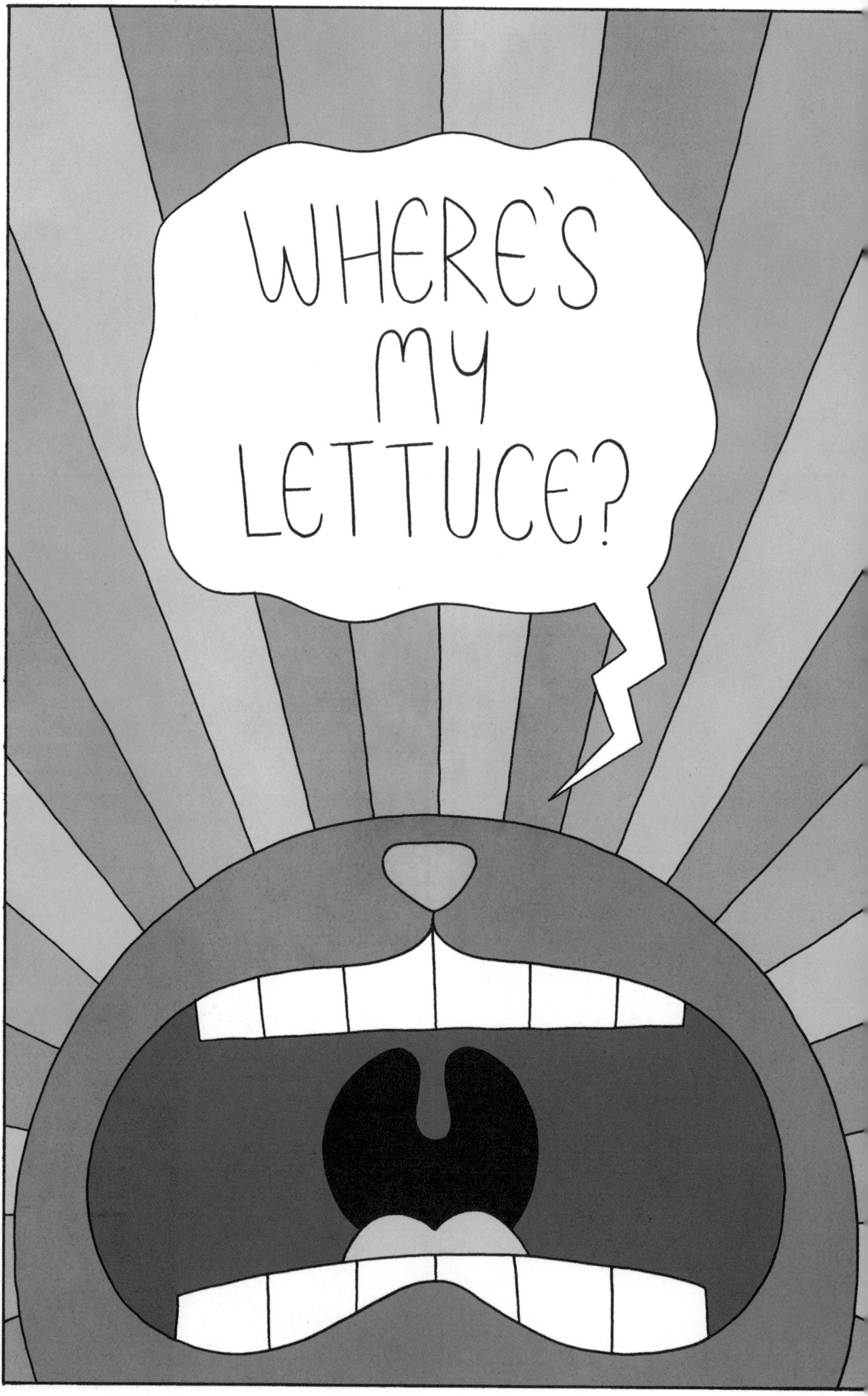
WHERE'S MY LETTUCE?

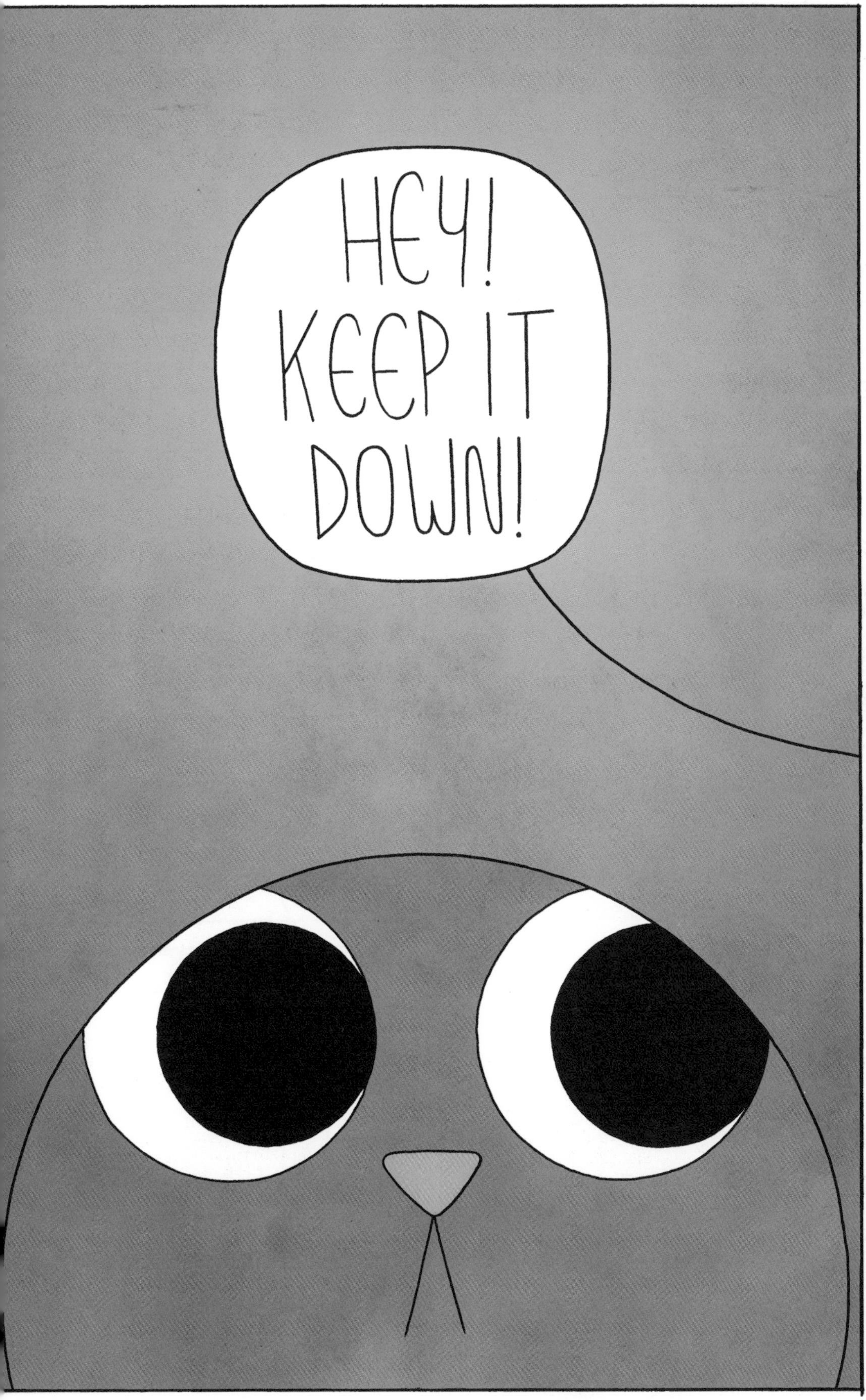
HEY! KEEP IT DOWN!

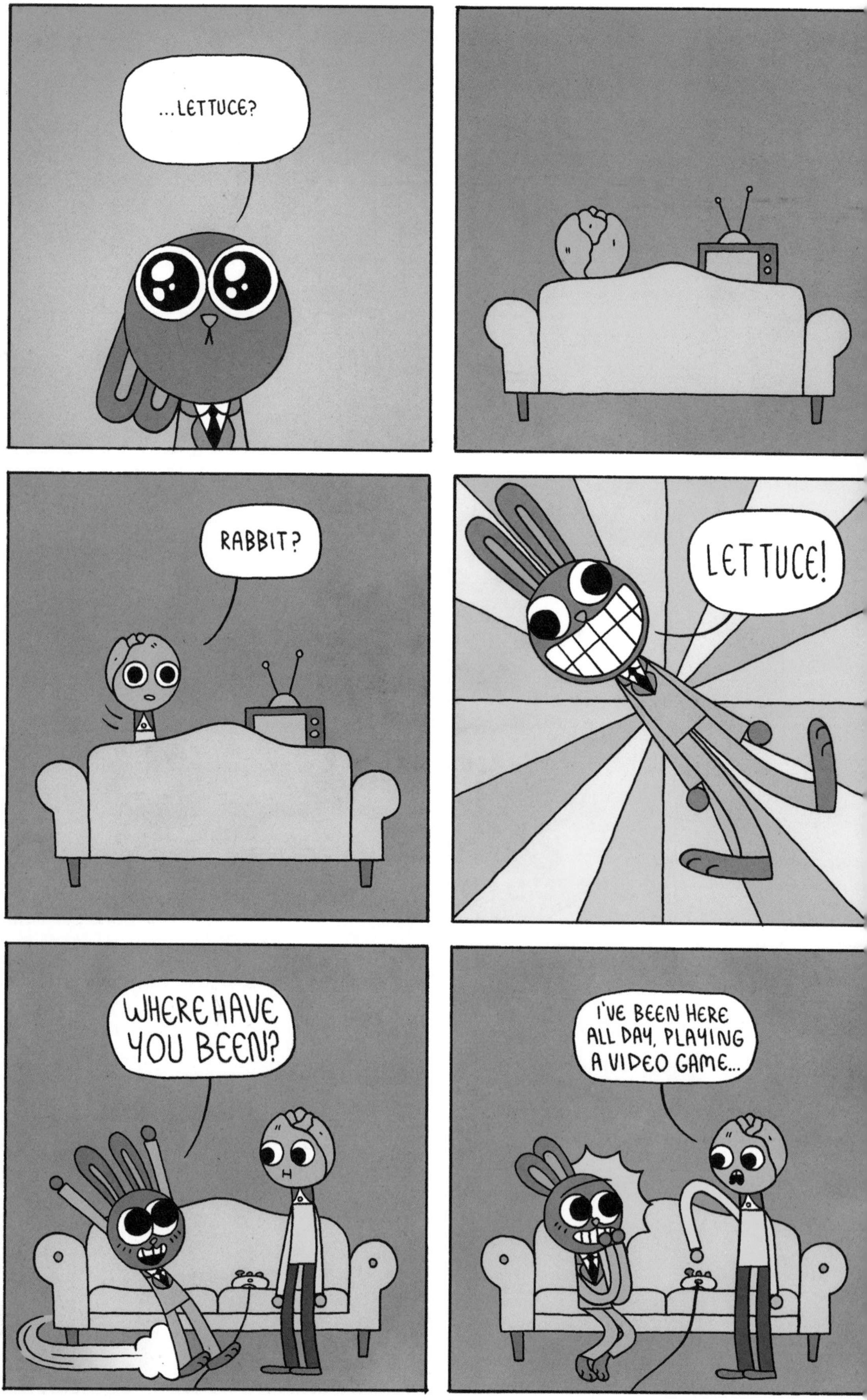
...LETTUCE?
RABBIT?
LETTUCE!
WHERE HAVE YOU BEEN?
I'VE BEEN HERE ALL DAY, PLAYING A VIDEO GAME...

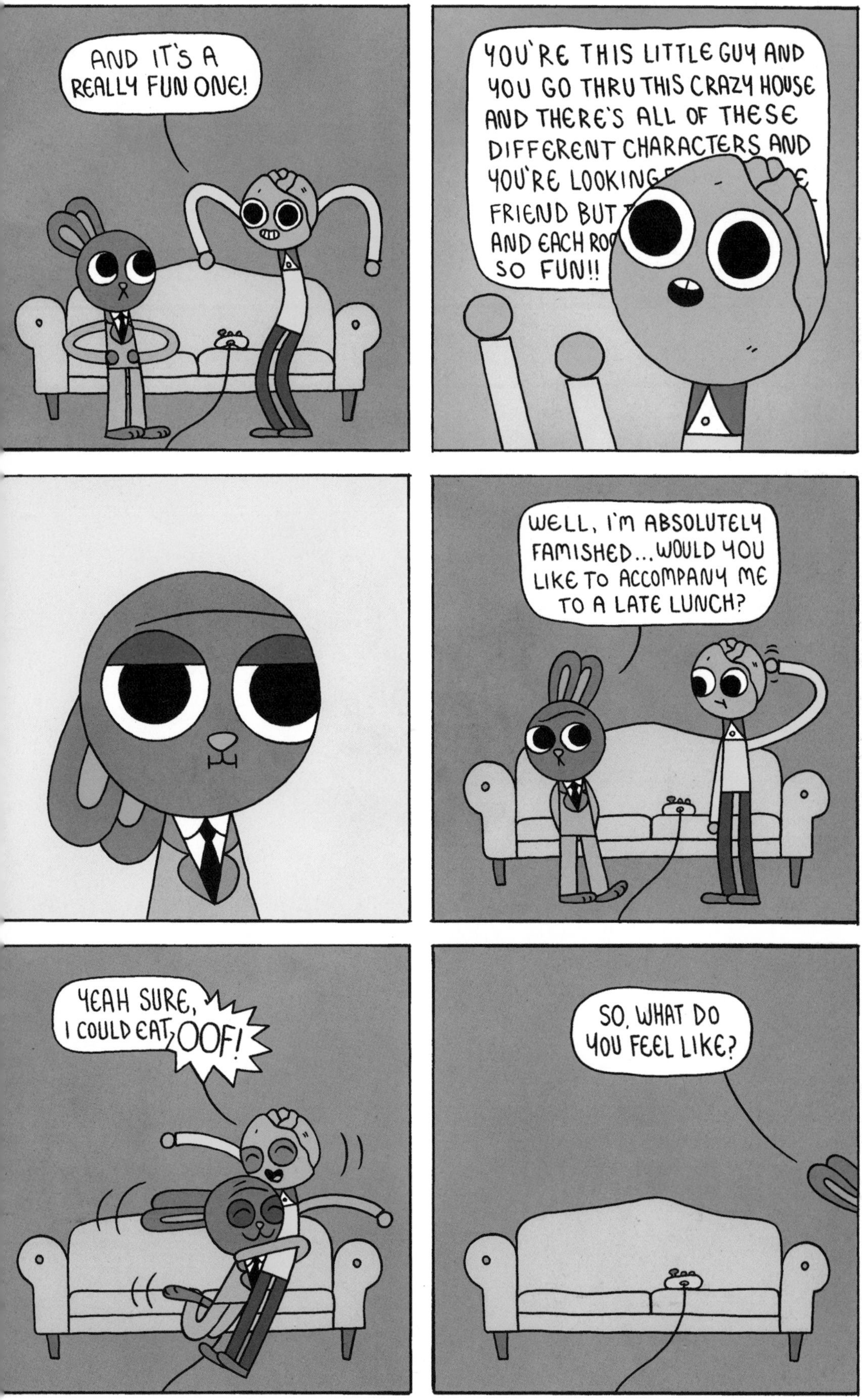
AND IT'S A REALLY FUN ONE!
YOU'RE THIS LITTLE GUY AND YOU GO THRU THIS CRAZY HOUSE AND THERE'S ALL OF THESE DIFFERENT CHARACTERS AND YOU'RE LOOKING
FRIEND BUT
AND EACH RO
SO FUN!!
WELL, I'M ABSOLUTELY FAMISHED... WOULD YOU LIKE TO ACCOMPANY ME TO A LATE LUNCH?
YEAH SURE, I COULD EAT,
OOF!
SO, WHAT DO YOU FEEL LIKE?

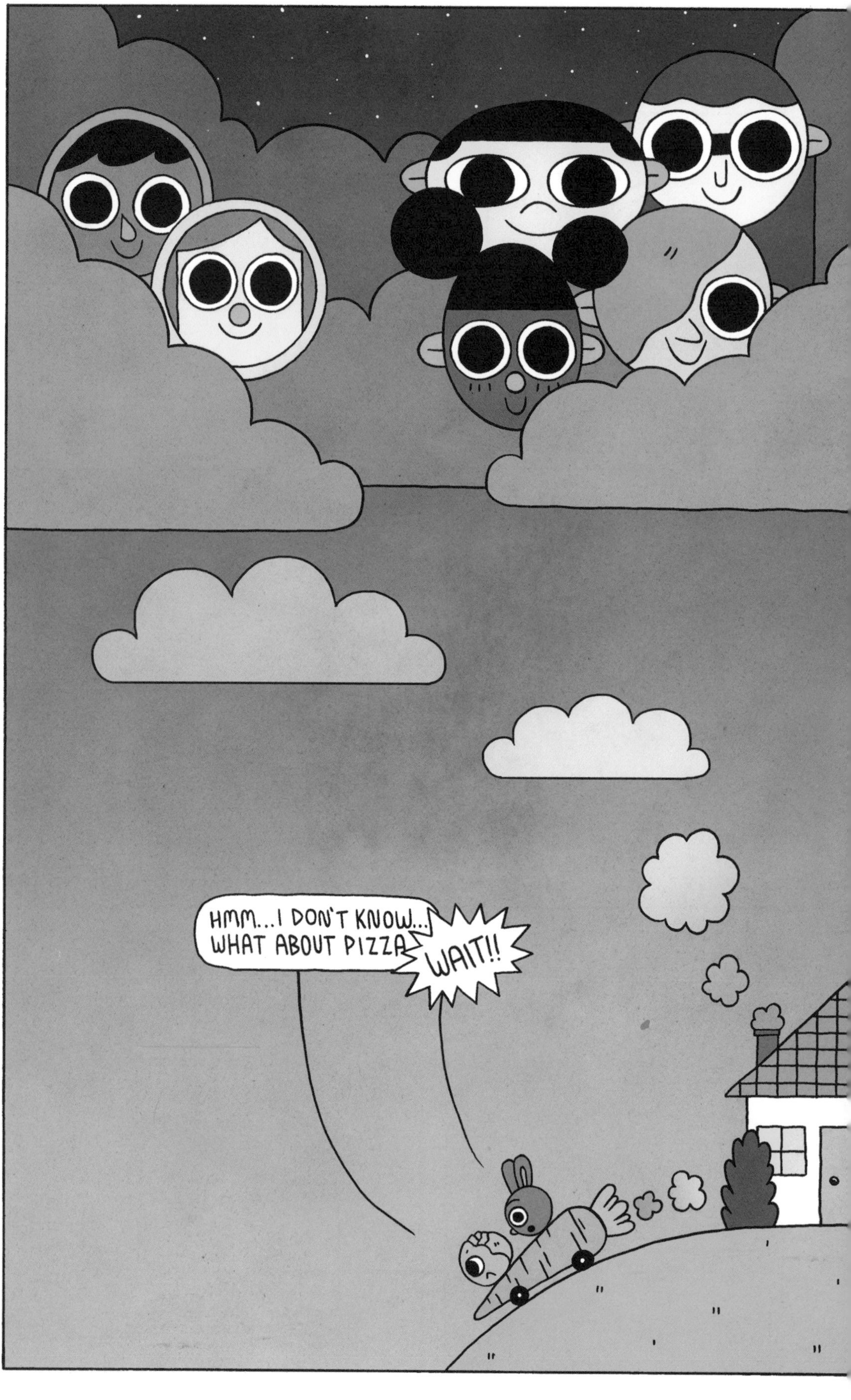
HMM...I DON'T KNOW... WHAT ABOUT PIZZA
WAIT!!

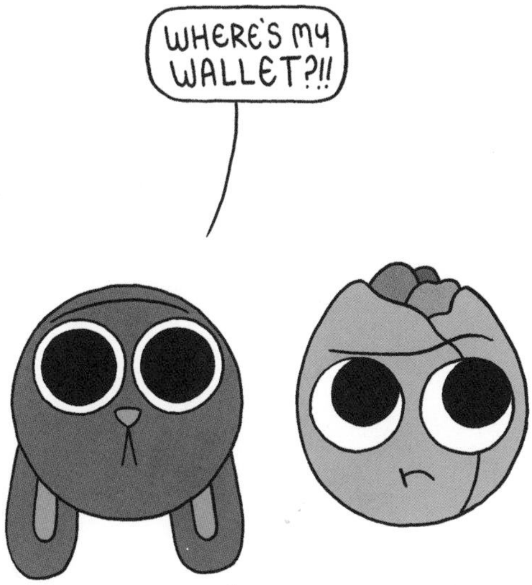
WHERE'S MY WALLET?!!

PUBLISHED BY KOYAMA PRESS
WWW.KOYAMAPRESS.COM
FIRST EDITION: MAY 2019
ISBN: 978-1-927668-65-8
PRINTED IN CHINA
KOYAMA PRESS GRATEFULLY ACKNOWLEDGES THE CANADA COUNCIL
FOR THE ARTS AND THE ONTARIO ARTS COUNCIL FOR THEIR SUPPORT
OF OUR PUBLISHING PROGRAM.